WHEN LOVE SOARS

Viva Espana, Book One

BARBARA MCMAHON

When Love Soars

This is a work of fiction. Names, characters, places and incidents are products of the author's imagination and are used fictitiously. Any resemblance to actual events, locales, organizations or persons living or dead is entirely coincidental.

Artificial Intelligence (AI) was not used to create any part of this book.

Chapter One

Abrienda Delmarico set the coffee tray down on the low table between the sofa and the visitor chairs. The two men were in deep discussion, hardly noticing her. She stepped back, wondering if her boss needed anything else.

A quick glance out the window showed the storm that had been threatening had arrived. Sheets of rain slid down the windows. It was so overcast it looked like dusk, though it was only late afternoon. She could hardly see the sea.

Sighing softly, she regretted the wet walk she'd have to take to get to the bus and then again after her stop for the three blocks to the flat. She'd be soaked and cold by the time she reached home tonight.

Still, it couldn't be helped. She had an umbrella, but the way the wind was driving the rain, she knew it would offer little shelter.

"Ha, in your dreams," Vincente Alvarez said, laughing sardonically at something his business rival said.

Abrienda turned to look at Domingo Ortego. What had he said to cause her boss's outburst? Not that Vincente Alvarez was the most complacent man. She'd worked for his firm more than seven years, and the last three of those for the head man himself. She knew how quickly he flew off the handle if aggravated.

"Care to wager fifty grand on it?" Domingo asked easily.

He leaned back casually in the chair, watching his rival with calculating eyes. Abrienda moved back a bit, preparing to leave, watching Domingo Ortego warily.

Despite being a trust-fund baby, Domingo had developed a thriving import-export business that was a major player in the Mediterranean area and was now moving globally, with offices around the world. He worked hard and played hard. Young to have achieved so much, he had the arrogance that went with amazing success.

When he walked into the office, she always felt a bit in awe. He wasted no time with chitchat with a lowly employee. He knew his worth and his time was valuable. Still, twice over the past several months she'd caught him studying her. When she'd met his gaze, he'd winked and looked away.

She watched him every chance she got. He was mesmerizing, fascinating. But if ever he caught her staring at him, she'd be mortified.

"You're on. And I'll delight in taking your check," Vincente replied with an arrogance equal to Domingo's.

Abrienda shifted her gaze to her boss. In his late fifties, he was always looking for new challenges to prove to the world he was still in top form. What was it about men that they had to constantly be in competition with each other?

"You're mistaken, it's I who will delight in taking yours," Domingo retorted.

Mid thirties, and gorgeous to boot, Domingo Ortego had risen in the ranks of important men in Barcelona with meteoric speed, which was why she'd seen him numerous times over the last three years. The only men her boss dealt with were the city's high rollers.

She'd also bet her last Euro that Domingo had never paid enough attention to her to recognize her on the street. A quick glance, eyes trailing over her trim figure, and then he'd move on.

Vincente picked up a cup of the hot coffee and poured cream in it, stirring gently. When the small ritual was complete, he looked at Domingo.

"You have only been ballooning a couple of years. You're a fool to think you can outrace me. I've been doing it for more than a decade."

"I'm a quick learner," Domingo said.

His easy grin captivated Abrienda's attention. What would it be like to have him smile at her that way?

"Or is that your way of trying to get out of the wager we just made?" Domingo taunted.

"I'm not trying to get out of anything," Vincente protested. "It'll be easy money."

"As will the deal we're about to sign. You are signing, are you not?"

Vincente looked at the contract that lay on the low table in front of him. "Should I have my attorneys review it once more?"

"They've had it for a week. Nothing's changed."

"So you say."

Domingo's easy manner dropped in a heartbeat. He narrowed his eyes as he studied Vincente.

He said slowly, "So I do say. Do you doubt my word?"

The silky tone of his voice belied the anger that showed

in the clenched jaw, the flashing dark eyes. He wouldn't be an adversary Abrienda wanted.

Vincente shrugged and sipped his coffee. After a swallow that had Abrienda wondering if he was playing with fire to delay his answer, he deliberately put the cup back on the saucer.

"I do not doubt your word. It's not a small deal that can be brushed away if it fails," Vincente explained.

"It will not fail," Domingo replied.

Vincente stared at Domingo for a long moment, then nodded. He took his pen and signed both sets of papers with a flourish.

Domingo wasn't quick to relax. Abrienda almost held her breath as the drama played out before her. Both men had forgotten she was in the room. She dare not move for worry of drawing their attention. She wished she could ease out the door and be gone.

Tossing his pen on the table, Vincente leaned back in his chair.

"How about we make the challenge a bit more interesting," he said.

"By?" Domingo asked, calmly reaching for the pen to sign his own name to the contracts.

"We'll limit people on board to ourselves and one guest—a nonballooner—chosen by the opposition. I choose who rides with you, you choose for me. We each have a man on the chase teams to keep the records in conjunction with the chase teams. We compete in the daily events at the festival and then begin our long jump."

Domingo considered the suggestion for a moment, then

with an obvious change in demeanor, relaxed, leaned back and smiled.

"That works for me. You'll be so far behind by the fourth day of the festival you'll concede without the long jump."

Vincente looked at Abrienda. "What do you think?"

She glanced at her boss's long-time rival and regretfully shook her head. Vincente wasn't one to concede defeat in anything.

"It'll never happen."

"Spoken like a true PA, loyal to the end," Vincente said with a grin. "You're my choice."

Abrienda stared at him in shock. "I know nothing about hot air balloons."

Only that they looked lovely when quietly sailing by, far overhead. And that it made her sick to even think about being so high above the ground.

"The purpose of the bet is to pit Domingo's skill, such as it may be, against mine. By each having a novice, we'll equalize the competition. One on one, so to speak," Vincente said.

"The Barcelona Balloon Festival will be four days of races and events. For us after day four we make a long jump and see who can get the farthest in a week. Are you up to that?" Domingo asked her.

She looked at him, feeling the full force of those dark eyes as he regarded her. She shivered. Spend eleven days with him in the confines of those little baskets that dangled beneath the balloons? Not likely.

"No. I can't do that. Pick someone else," she said to her boss. She knew nothing about the sport, but she knew she feared heights. To spend days in the air was more than she could deal with. Not to mention spending all that time alone with Domingo Ortego.

The man was beyond gorgeous—tall and masculine, his dark hair shone beneath the artificial light. At thirty-four he had no gray marring the rich mahogany color. His dark eyes mirrored his emotions—when he wanted them to. Moving from amusement to anger in a split second, he fascinated her when she was around him—which wasn't often, thank goodness. He drew her involuntary interest like a flame drew a moth. And she'd expect the same results if she let herself be drawn in—instant annihilation.

He was one of the best-looking men she'd ever seen. Everyone thought so. Especially the society photographers who loved to have him on their pages—usually escorting a beautiful woman to some high-society event.

Of course they also captured him racing his yacht last summer and when he won the single-engine airplane race from Cadiz to Barcelona two years ago.

He participated in a wide and wild range of sports. She'd seen the spreads in the Sunday newspapers and read with fascinated interest, since she could claim a brief acquaintance with him because of his dealings with her boss.

But she had no desire to spend even an hour in his company. He was far too dynamic and flamboyant to have anything in common with her. He'd find her boring and predictable and probably amusing.

With all the adulation he received, he was undoubtedly self-centered and self-focused. Did he ever approach life like a normal person—with worries and concerns? Probably not. Having the Ortego fortune behind him didn't hurt, either.

"Yes, Alvarez, pick someone else," Domingo agreed, turning away from Abrienda.

"Like the woman you're dating now?" Vincente asked sardonically. "Maybe I should. You'd lose track of even the basics with the charm Teresa offers and I'd win easily. But I'd rather have a challenge."

"Teresa would dislike the early hours and the discomfort when it's cold. How do I know a person of your choice wouldn't sabotage the race?"

"I would never do such a thing," Abrienda exclaimed, incensed.

How dare he impugn her integrity.

He shrugged and took one of the contracts, putting it into his briefcase.

"Second choice?" he asked Alvarez.

"I'll get back to you."

"I think I'll ask my PA to join you. Helena at least follows the sport, though she has never participated in any events. I gave her a ride last year and she liked it."

"Send me her name and phone number and I'll talk to her," Vincente said. "And I'll have one of my chase crew contact yours. There will be no sabotage. He'll help as a regular crew member—only be there to verify the times and distances."

"Do we get rights of refusal?" Domingo asked.

"If both agree," Vincente replied.

"Then start writing your check," Domingo said, deliberately goading the other man.

Abrienda thought about the report that still needed finishing. She didn't have time to stand around and listen to two very wealthy men talk about a silly hot air balloon race. The fifty thousand Euros they bandied around so easily would make a world of difference in her life. To most people's lives. To these men it was chump change. Betting on a balloon race seemed frivolous in the extreme.

"Maybe we should sweeten the pot a bit. Loser has to present to winner in front of the Barcelona Business Alliance at the next quarterly meeting," Domingo suggested.

Abrienda looked at Domingo, seeing the devilment in his eyes. He was wild and daring, and she strongly suspected he loved every moment of this.

It was obvious he never expected to lose; he rarely did. Not only did he have pots of money, he had the best luck in the world, if the newspapers could be believed. From learning to fly a few years ago, to deep sea diving, to this newest hobby of hot air ballooning, he loved to challenge himself—and anyone involved in the sport with him.

Vincente gathered his copy of the contract and held it out for Abrienda. She stepped closer to take it and then retreated to the door of his office.

Standing, Vincente held out his hand to Domingo.

"May the best man win, and I intend to!"

Domingo stood, as well, and shook his hand.

"Prepare your presentation speech for the BBA's meeting. It had better be good, to wipe out the sting of humiliation."

Abrienda opened the door for the departing man. When Domingo drew level with her, he looked at her again.

"It's not too late to change your mind," he said. "Find out what working with a winner is like."

"My boss will win," she said loyally.

He shook his head and winked at her before walking past. She could smell the expensive aftershave lotion he used—something fresh and woodsy. Perfect for him. She felt the attraction that seemed like an invisible aura around him and for a split second she wished that wink had meant something special.

When Domingo Ortego left her anteroom and walked toward the elevators, she turned and looked at her boss. While not as notorious as his competitor, he could still claim outrageous behavior and daring escapades that made the papers. How his wife stood it all these years was a mystery to Abrienda.

She looked at her boss. “Can you win?” she asked.

“Of course,” he said easily. Walking back to his desk, he looked at her. “But I need your help. I want you to go with Ortego.”

She shook her head. “I’m afraid of heights. Besides, what would I talk to the man about?”

He laughed. “No need to worry about that. He’ll be too busy trying to outmaneuver me. Don’t worry about receiving a pass from the man, you aren’t his type. He likes luscious, sophisticated prima donnas, not hardworking businesswomen. The intent is to make sure he isn’t getting help from a ringer.”

Abrienda shook her head again. She couldn’t go off on a hot air balloon ride. Even if she didn’t have a phobia about heights, she had work to do. Her brother to take care of. She’d have to find a way to convince Vincente it would be a mistake. He was too focused on the need to one-up Domingo Ortego to worry about a mere personal assistant’s reasons for refusing.

"I need to get the Tunisia report finished. And you need to think of another choice. I really can't do it."

Turning, she headed for the door.

"Then call Teresa Valquez for me, will you?" he asked. "I might get her interested. Maybe she'd distract Domingo long enough for me to have an easy triumph."

Abrienda nodded and kept walking. Teresa Valquez was Domingo's latest girlfriend. Abrienda had recently read about them attending a reception together. The accompanying picture had captured the worldly look of his latest. Her sleek, short blond hair contrasted so well with her dark eyes. The gown she'd worn was the latest fashion and had looked fabulous on her figure.

Except, would she still be around by the time the balloon race began? The one thing Abrienda had noticed was how frequently Domingo changed companions. The balloon race was still a couple of weeks away—plenty of time for him to find a new woman and for Teresa to be old news.

She sat at her desk and looked up the phone number for Ms. Valquez. When she was on the line, Abrienda clicked her over to Vincente's phone. She could finish the report if she had no more interruptions before close of business.

Just before five, she stapled the last set and put them in the envelopes for different staff members. That was a major project completed. The rest of the week should be a breeze—or as much as it ever was working for Vincente Alvarez.

She liked her job well enough; she found it interesting and fulfilling. Which was good, since she'd likely be at it for another four or five years. Once her brother was out of college and on his own, she'd give a thought to returning to school to work for her own degree—interrupted barely months after she'd started university by the death of her parents.

Abrienda's goal remained to become a graphic designer—working with multinational corporations to develop and maintain web pages. She loved playing around on computers. She'd streamlined many of the office functions through technology. But it wasn't enough to satisfy her. She wanted new horizons. She dabbled in web design for friends, utilizing the latest in AI technology. But she constantly looked for more challenges and a monetary reward for her work.

When she'd expressed that interest to Vincente a couple of years ago, asking if she could switch divisions, he'd refused. He hadn't wanted to break in another new PA. Maybe she did her job too well, but it wasn't in her to do less than her best.

At least she had a good position that enabled her and her brother to live in a modest flat. After their parents were killed, there'd been more debt than assets. Once everything had been sold, there was nothing left for extras.

Abrienda still remembered the panic she felt knowing that Jose depended entirely on her. She'd only been nineteen, Jose a mere eight. She'd floundered those first couple of years until she began to work for this firm.

Promotions had moved her up and her current job now paid enough to save a bit for college for her younger brother. One more year of public school and he'd be off to university. He wanted to be a physicist. He'd probably be over the moon with a chance to ride in a hot air balloon. She dare not tell him. He'd badger her forever to take advantage of the opportunity.

She shut off her computer, tidied her desk and donned her serviceable raincoat. She was already planning the evening meal she'd prepare for herself and Jose.

Vincente stepped into her office.

"I need you to renew my order of weather schedules first thing in the morning."

He handed her a piece of paper on which he'd written down the Internet addresses. One was from a local weather forecasting service in Barcelona. The other two covered other areas, including the eastern part of Spain and parts of southern France.

She nodded. "Anything else?"

"Not right now. I've got to prepare for the flight, though. There's more to it this time than casual fun. I can't wait to see Domingo's face in front of the BBA giving me the winning check."

"The entire plan sounds scary," she murmured.

She'd gone to the Barcelona Balloon Festival the first time it had been held after she joined the firm. She hadn't stayed after the first wave of balloons lifted into the air. The small wicker baskets were dwarfed by the huge balloons, dangling by incredibly thin ropes that connected the basket to the balloon.

Imagine rising above the earth dependent solely on hot air in a large nylon bag. She shuddered just thinking about it. The entire venture looked precarious and dangerous. She preferred to keep her feet on terra firma.

"It's perfectly safe and a lot of fun. There's nothing like soaring a couple of thousand feet above the earth. Watching the landscape drift by below, going where the wind takes you."

"Unless you get tangled in power lines and get zapped, or go down in the Med and drown before rescue, or—"

Or just fall from the basket and splat on the ground. She shook her head at the horrible image that popped into her mind.

"That happens, like, once in a lifetime." Vincente laughed.

"It could be *your* lifetime or the end of it!"

"No, I don't think so. I haven't had even so much as a near miss in all the years I've been doing this. Anyway, you're off the hook. Teresa Valquez is delighted to be going with Domingo. I think she expects a ring on her finger by the end of the trip. Doubt he'll ask, though, because he hasn't so far. He strikes me as the perpetual playboy bachelor who's having far too much fun to get tied down. See you in the morning," he added, turning and reentering his office.

She grabbed her umbrella, wondering if that or her raincoat would be much protection against the deluge that continued.

Stepping outside a few moments later, Abrienda paused beneath the building's portico debating whether or not to dash to the bus stop without her umbrella raised and hope she didn't become soaked, or give in to the inevitable and use the umbrella until the wind turned it inside out.

A sleek black sports car drew to a stop at the curb in front of her. The passenger window slid down.

"Need a lift?"

She leaned over a bit to peer in. Domingo Ortego looked back at her.

"Get in, I'll drive you home," he ordered.

Normally Abrienda would object to his imperious tone, but she was pragmatic enough to appreciate a ride in the storm. She quickly got into the car as the window slid up.

"Why?" she asked as she fastened her seat belt.

"To get to know you, of course."

As the car pulled back into traffic, Abrienda sighed softly. The luxurious leather interior even smelled like wealth. The seat cushioned her lovingly and she surreptitiously rubbed her fingers against its softness.

"There's no need. Vincente got Teresa Valquez to agree to accompany you on the balloon race. I won't be going."

Would he let her off at the next corner now that there was no need to become better acquainted?

"Damn, I don't know which is worse, you or Teresa," he said, moving to another lane as traffic began to get heavy.

"Thanks a lot," she murmured, not feeling kindly toward the man. She fervently hoped he lost the race to her boss just to take him down a peg or two.

"They say 'better the devil you know,' but I'm not so sure. I do know Teresa and the spin she's sure to put on this. You're an unknown, but at least I know you have no ulterior motive."

"I'm not going, so there's no more to say," Abrienda said firmly.

"Still, I'm not dumping you in the rain. Where to?"

She lived in an older section of town, with lots of flats and small markets, winding streets and little parking. Nothing like the palatial home he must live in surrounded by gardens and giving a stupendous view of the city and the Med.

"It's off Via Estrada," she said.

"So what's Alvarez's game plan?" he asked a moment later, easily driving in the rainy evening twilight.

"He wants to win," Abrienda pointed out dryly.

"So do I," Domingo said.

"He thinks you'll be distracted by Ms. Valquez and that

will give him the edge," she said, hoping to startle him.

Domingo glanced at her a second. "Honest. Hmm…unusual."

"Then you must hang out with the wrong people," she snapped.

First he considered she would sabotage his race, now he seemed surprised to find her an honest person. The nerve of the man! She clutched her purse tighter, hoping she could hold on to her temper until she reached home.

"Touchy, too. I bet there's temper in there somewhere," he mocked. "But being the perfect little personal assistant to Alvarez, I'm sure you've damped that down a lot."

She wanted to say something pithy to knock him off his high horse, but nothing came to mind. She hated that.

"Do *you* think Teresa would distract me?" he asked, turning onto Via Estrada.

"I have no idea," she replied stiffly.

His affair with the beautiful woman was none of her business. She refused to speculate based on the innuendos of the press.

"If you and my boss have to have a stupid race, I suspect one distraction would be equal to another."

"So maybe I should find a beautiful woman to ride with him."

Abrienda said nothing. Domingo had to know Vincente was married. Did he think Vincente would be unfaithful to his wife for a balloon race?

"No thoughts?" he pressed.

"None you want to hear," she murmured. "Turn at the second traffic signal, right. Then three blocks to Via Escondido."

"Maybe I do want to hear," he said.

She hesitated a moment, but knowing she was almost home, she felt reckless.

"It's that stupid bet. Don't you think the two of you could find better use for that much money than betting it against each other? There are hungry children, sick people, homeless in the world who could benefit."

"I give to charity," he protested.

He couldn't see it. His type never would. She shook her head. He lived so differently from the masses.

"Tell you what," he said. "I'll turn over my winnings to your favorite charity. You just name it and I'll sign the check right over."

She looked at him in astonishment. "Why would you do such a thing?"

"Why not? The money isn't the important part of the wager, the winning is."

Abrienda turned to look out at the street. She couldn't imagine carelessly dismissing fifty thousand Euros.

When he reached her apartment building a few minutes later, he stopped in front and looked up through the windshield. The building was old, but still interesting, with stonework embellishments and tall windows.

"Is the inside also old or has it been renovated?"

"The building is almost a hundred years old, so of course the inside has been renovated."

About fifty years ago, but Abrienda saw no need to tell him that.

He looked at her. "I'm sorry you won't be going with me. I love a challenge."

Abrienda frowned. "I'd be no challenge."

"Getting you on my side would be the challenge. Teammates should share the goal. Would you throw your heart into my race or hamper it at every turn?"

"We'll never know, will we?" she asked.

He was so close she could see the faint lines radiating from the corners of his eyes. See the deep-brown irises that almost melded into the black pupils.

He rubbed a finger lightly down her cheek.

"Seems a shame."

She jerked back. "Thank you for the ride," she said hastily, throwing open the door and scrambling from the car.

She made a quick dash to the front door and hardly felt the rain. She was churning with the emotional onslaught of his touch that had her insides turning to mush. He was wrong—she'd be no challenge to him at all if he ever turned his attentions on her.

She turned and watched as he tooted the horn and drove away, puddles splashing from the wheels. Long after the taillights had merged into traffic, she gazed after the sleek black dream machine. She didn't even own a car. Not that she needed the expense as the bus served her perfectly well. She and Jose had a nice flat, nothing like the home she'd grown up in, but the best she could afford. Her job was good and in only a few years she'd be able to return to her own education.

Opening the door to the flat, she saw she'd beaten Jose home, probably because of the ride Domingo had given her. She'd start dinner then change. Afterward, she would read up on what she could find on the Internet about hot air balloons. She knew only the rudimentary facts about the sport, which she'd gleaned from Vincente's enthusiastic discussion when he returned from some ballooning event.

She did know long jumps meant trips beyond the one-to three-hour ones near a festival site. They were rarer than the gathering of balloonists in favorite spots like Barcelona or London or Albuquerque, New Mexico, in America. Those races followed some prescribed activities, like waves of balloons in the morning flights or just before sunset. They also required a chase crew to pick them up when they came down. If there were competitions, it was usually dropping beanbags in target sites. Points went to those who dropped the closest to the center or who dropped earlier rather than later.

Once in comfortable and warm sweats, Abrienda turned on her computer. She told herself she was learning about the sport to talk more knowledgeably with her boss. But she also searched for what would fascinate a dynamic man like Domingo Ortego. Doing a search on his name, she began to read about his life. Some aspects she knew, other items were new. A complete dossier online. Did he know people could find out so much merely by tapping a few keys on a computer?

Despite her own reservations about flight, she wondered a bit wistfully what it would be like to sail soundlessly over the countryside, going where the wind blew, seeing farms and towns from the air with a man who made life seem more exciting than anything she'd experienced.

His own parents were divorced. According to one source, he maintained "cordial relationships" with both, whatever that meant. She missed her parents all the time. She couldn't imagine having mere "cordial relationships" with them.

"Hola, I'm home," Jose called.

So much for dreaming about hot air balloon rides and sexy billionaires who took to the air. Reality returned. She had dinner to finish.

Chapter Two

Domingo let himself into the empty house from the garage. It was raining like a monsoon outside. The house was dark and a bit chilled. He flipped on the switch to illuminate the mudroom, then stepped into the hall. Turning on lights as he walked back to the kitchen, he considered the bet he'd made.

Then he almost laughed remembering the outrage of Alvarez's prim PA when he'd suggested she might sabotage his flight.

He didn't know what had made him drive back by Alvarez's office building at the end of the working day. He'd wanted to talk to Abrienda to see if he could glean any information to explain why Alvarez suggested she be part of his crew.

It made even less sense now that he knew Teresa was going with him. What was Alvarez's thinking? He couldn't seriously suppose that Teresa would distract Domingo from his goal of winning the race?

The short car ride with Abrienda hadn't given him much insight except he now knew she deplored the bet for altruistic financial reasons. But she didn't seem to have a special interest in Alvarez's winning. Or his losing.

But she intrigued Domingo for other reasons. She seemed as jumpy as a cat with dogs baying. He'd caught her watching him the few times he'd actually gone to Alvarez's office. Domingo was used to that from women, but she never flirted with him, never acknowledged any interest besides the looks he'd feel from time to time. If he glanced her way, her eyes would already be moving away.

What made her tick? He'd given her even more reason for Alvarez to lose by promising his winnings to her favorite charity. An offer which she hadn't jumped on. That puzzled him as well. Most people he knew would instantly come up with a name or cause to gain that much money.

Vincente Alvarez had long been a thorn in his side, ever since he'd made a rather underhanded maneuver five years ago that had cost Domingo time and money. Domingo would delight in showing up the man in front of the Business Alliance. Vincente had been the only ballooner in the group until Domingo took up the sport.

Alvarez liked to brag, but those bragging rights would be curtailed when Domingo beat him—especially since he was the newcomer to the sport.

The bet presented a new personal challenge as well—piloting a balloon farther afield. The trick would be with the weather and getting an ongoing reliable way to indicate the wind factor.

How much fuel could he carry to keep airborne longer, without being too much weight for lift? The logistics suddenly seemed daunting enough to fire up his determination not only to beat Alvarez, but to try for a new record.

Domingo smiled. He loved pitting his own resources against others. He could already see himself standing in front of the BBA and accepting Vincente's check. That he'd now promised to turn it over to charity didn't bother him. The entire bet was not about the money, but about proving to Vincente Alvarez that he wasn't the only one in Barcelona with the *cojones* to venture into the unknown.

Their balloons could end up over the Pyrenees or over the Med. He briefly wondered if they could get to Africa. No, that was unlikely as this time of year the prevailing winds blew north and west.

Opening the oven, he savored the aroma of the casserole his housekeeper had prepared and set in the oven before she left for home. It wouldn't be done for another half hour. He was home earlier than usual, having left work to get to Alvarez's building early enough to catch Abrienda.

The house phone rang and Domingo picked up the kitchen extension.

"Ortego," he said.

"Hola," Teresa said in her sultry voice.

"Teresa," he acknowledged.

He wasn't expecting to hear from her tonight. Was she calling about the race?

"It's raining and I'm bored," she said. "It's too wet to go out and there's nothing on television. No friends want to venture forth to visit me."

He could hear the pout in her voice. Picture her lush red lips in a moue that invited kissing.

"Unless you do," she finished.

He liked Teresa. They had fun together when they went out. But he didn't relish becoming a frequent visitor at her home. That led to ideas that he was definitely not pursuing. She knew that.

"Not tonight. It's pouring and I just got home. Besides, I need to start planning for the race. I heard Alvarez called you and you're going with me."

"Won't that be delightful, just the two of us in the gondola of the balloon, riding high above the crowds?"

"Delightful," he replied sardonically.

Did she have any idea what was involved? If she thought they'd enjoy a tryst, he had better explain the facts of balloon racing.

"Ohhh, I could come there and plan the race with you," she said, as if it were a sudden idea.

"I thought you didn't want to go out into the rain," he said, loosening his tie.

He wanted to look at maps covering all the possible directions the balloon might go on the long jump, get a head start on preparing for the event. He didn't have time to entertain anyone.

"If I get a taxi there, I won't get very wet," she almost purred.

"Not tonight, babe. I've got work to do."

"Honestly, Domingo, you need to slow down a bit and enjoy all that money you make."

Or let you enjoy it, he thought cynically. He knew the women he dated were attracted to his money and his notoriety. Normally it didn't bother him but tonight it did.

If he were a pauper, would Teresa even look at him? Not in a million years. Much less invite him to her home.

Unexpectedly the image of Alvarez's PA flashed into his mind. Abrienda would probably do more than look at him if he were a pauper, she'd try to help him find a job and a place to live. Get money from the rich to help out the poor.

Great, he was either a charity case or a meal ticket, which didn't paint a very complimentary picture of him either way. Had that been what his father faced? He hadn't stuck with marriage for long.

Unlike his mother who reveled in the state, if five husbands to date were any indication.

Domingo didn't like the way he was thinking. Reminders of his parents always fed his frustration. He'd felt the odd man out in his family from the first time he'd been sent away to boarding school. His father was too busy to care for a child and his mother was always concentrating on attracting her next husband to devote much time to her two sons. They would have done better not to have had children in the first place.

But then he wouldn't be here, nor his brother, so maybe it hadn't been all bad. But he had no plans for marriage for a long time—if ever.

"I've got to go. How about dinner tomorrow night?" he offered, to placate her.

There was a pause, then Teresa accepted. She wanted to talk longer, but he soon ended the conversation.

He had time to change into casual clothes before the casserole would be ready. He wanted to begin his study of the weather patterns and wind flows he might expect to find when making the long balloon trip. He liked planning strategy almost as much as implementation.

He enjoyed the flights he made with the balloon. Work kept him busier than he might like during the summer months, yet when time permitted, he'd take a sail in the balloon. He had several friends who volunteered for the chase team, in exchange for rides.

It occurred to him as he climbed the stairs that spending every day for a week or longer with Teresa might be more than he could take. She was fun an evening at a time, but how would she hold up to hours in the basket with the harsh sound of the burners going on and off? Or with the unexpected accommodations they'd have to make for the nights when they touched down who knew where? It wasn't like a normal holiday trip where they could phone ahead for reservations. Or festivals, where they knew where they were to put down each day, with the chase team already on-site.

They'd have to bed down wherever the balloon landed and be up early to get the dawn sky. He planned to beat Alvarez so there would be no time to look for the amenities she was used to.

He couldn't picture Teresa lasting. Was that Alvarez's hope—rather than Teresa distracting him, she might abandon him? What would Domingo do if Teresa didn't stay the course? He refused to forfeit, that he knew, even if he had to tie her to the gondola for the race.

Or take Alvarez's PA as a substitute.

As he changed into dark jeans and a dark sweater,

Domingo thought about Abrienda. She lived in an old building in an older section of town. She hadn't gushed about him giving her a ride. He almost smiled. Instead she'd berated him for squandering all that money on a bet.

And she'd looked outraged when he touched her cheek. Her skin had felt warm and soft. Though she hid it behind a prickly exterior, she was a very feminine woman.

She still hadn't said which charity she'd like the payment to go to. He'd have to contact her again to find out. Not that he needed an excuse to call most women, but with this one it would probably be wiser.

Chapter Three

As the day of the Barcelona Balloon Festival drew closer, work became totally chaotic for Abrienda. She had a dozen things to do each day in preparing for her boss's part in the event.

In addition to the normal business of the company, she had to line up the chase team, verify that the balloon was in top shape, work out various logistical scenarios to try to anticipate where the winds would drive the balloon each day on the long jump and field a dozen calls from Mrs. Alvarez, who was enjoying all the social activity associated with the Balloon Festival.

She was tired each night but, oddly enough, also exhilarated.

For once all aspects of the race were of interest. She listened more than she had for other events, soaking up every bit of information. That she knew two of the participants spurred her on.

"Abrienda, where are today's weather reports?" Vincente called out, two days before the festival started.

"I put them on your desk, left-hand side," she yelled back, not leaving her desk as she tried to finish the last of the meal planning. The four members of the chase team required a lot of food as they followed the balloon from the ground. No time to stop for meals or they'd lose sight of it and then have to rely on communications from Vincente in the balloon to find it again before it touched down.

She knew her boss would want snacks to eat while airborne each day and bottles of water to drink. She hadn't met Helena Marisol, but the two of them had spoken on the phone several times. She seemed excited about the trip and talked glowingly of her boss.

A couple of times during the week, Abrienda almost regretted she wouldn't be going with him. But the mere thought of being that high with nothing but air beneath her had her nerves fluttering.

The trick was to get good food that required little preparation. The only fire on the balloon would be the burners. Suddenly she stifled a giggle imagining the immaculate Ms. Valquez toasting a hot dog in the flames of Domingo Ortego's balloon burners.

It was far more likely he'd arrange for caviar and champagne for a snack.

She stopped for a moment, trying to picture Teresa even in the balloon. It was mind-boggling. From what Vincente said, the balloonist had to pay attention to the wind to get the maximum speed. Adjusting the height of the balloon to take advantage of different wind speeds took concentration. Vincente's rival would not be available to flirt with Teresa. Not if he was serious about winning.

Did she realize that? Abrienda knew Domingo would focus absolutely on winning the race rather than on the dubious delights of his passenger.

Abrienda shook her head. That wasn't her problem.

It was Thursday. Saturday morning was the first event of the festival. Even as early as Tuesday, she'd begun seeing hot air balloons drifting by as balloonists from all over the world came to compete, show off and enjoy themselves. Foreigners were trying to get a feel for the locale and the winds before the festival officially opened.

Twice she'd stood at her window for long moments watching balloons drift lazily over the sea. If she didn't have a fear of heights, would she enjoy taking a ride in one?

"They're pretty, aren't they?" Vincente asked, joining her at the window late in the afternoon. "You'll have to come to see us off."

"Helena called a little while ago. She wanted to know if she should line up anything special for the long jump."

"I think I'll thank Domingo's PA at my acceptance speech when I get his check," Vincente said thoughtfully. "She's committed to being the perfect passenger. I wonder how Ortego is faring with Teresa Valquez?"

He laughed at the thought.

"You're pretty sure you're going to win. What if you don't?"

She wouldn't relish working the week or so after such a loss. Her boss was not fun to be around when in a bad temper.

"I will. I never even consider defeat."

"Helena says Domingo is saying the same thing."

"Ha, he'll eat my dust."

Abrienda didn't operate that way. She always had a plan B in case plan A didn't work.

"You and Jose come to the field on Saturday to see us

off. Check in at the gate to find out where we'll be," her boss said.

She looked up at that. "Do you need me there?"

"No, but I thought you might like to see us fill the envelope and lift off. Marguerite says that's her favorite part," he said, mentioning his wife.

"The envelope," she repeated, remembering the explanation she had read on the Internet.

"The balloon. The nylon part is called the envelope. Then there's the basket or gondola and the burners. It's not rocket science, but I enjoy it."

"If the weather's nice, we might come. I know Jose would love it. Of course, he'll be explaining to me all about the physics that makes the lighter-than-air balloon fly with the added weight in the basket."

She loved her younger brother, but sometimes he left her in bewilderment discussing how things worked.

* * *

Saturday was a beautiful day. A bit on the cool side but perfect, as there were no clouds and only a brisk cool breeze blowing in from the Mediterranean Sea. Jose had been talking about the balloon festival ever since Abrienda had told him they would attend.

Vincente had instructed her to arrive at dawn as the balloons would be taking off very early. There were special buses from Barcelona to the festival, running on a frequent schedule.

Once she got to the large field a few miles outside of

Barcelona, Abrienda was caught up in the excitement. She and Jose checked in at the gate and received a map of the field, and the grid where her boss had his balloon. She and her brother set off down the area between the balloons. There were well over a hundred, all in various stages of being inflated. Fans pumped air in the inflation process. Once the balloon was more than half full, the burners began. The noise from the burners was surprisingly loud as they were fired up to heat the air in the envelope. Men and women were working, talking, laughing.

"Come to see me off?"

Abrienda looked to her left and saw Domingo Ortego. His balloon was halfway inflated, the bright red and stark black striking in the early-morning light. The basket lay on its side, two people at the opening of the envelope holding it wide for the fan to pump in air.

His attire matched the balloon, an all-black jumpsuit with a splash of red traversing his chest on the jacket. The colors suited him. The suit would keep him comfortable at the higher elevations and he could shed the jacket as the day warmed.

"Actually I came to see my boss off," she said, her eyes taking in all the activity around his balloon.

"A man can pretend," he said, flashing a smile at Jose. "I'm Domingo Ortego," he said, extending his hand.

Jose shook it, introducing himself. "This is great. Can I see your balloon and watch how it inflates? I read up about the entire process."

"Sure, come on over."

Abrienda stared after the two as they walked away. Jose shouldn't be asking Domingo a dozen questions. The man was the competition. Vincente would surely be glad to give Jose answers to anything he could come up with.

She started after them to rein in her brother, but they quickly outdistanced her, and before she caught up, Jose was actually at the side of the gondola, studying the burner apparatus with Domingo right at his side instructing. Members of his chase team joked back and forth, the atmosphere growing more festive.

She watched, glad, despite her misgivings, that Domingo was taking time to explain everything so thoroughly. Vincente would probably glossed over the details.

Jose missed their dad more than anything. He'd been a wonderful father, and the wound his loss had created would never be completely healed.

With work and keeping their apartment and all, Abrienda didn't date seriously. She had to wait for any permanent commitment until her brother was no longer her responsibility. So there was not a steady male influence in Jose's life. Had that been a mistake? Should she have tried to get married to provide him with that adult male exposure?

She looked around her. The noise level was growing. There were five long rows of balloons all being inflated, and the roaring sound the burners made filled the air. The bright colors were highlighted slightly by the flames, appearing to glow in the early dawn light.

Looking back, she drew on her patience to wait until Jose had enough information so they could continue to Vincente's balloon, still another half dozen farther along.

Suddenly a long flame shot out of the burners of Domingo's balloon, the noise startling. Jose was grinning,

Domingo by his side, watching as the flame shot into the balloon, the two helpers holding the mouth of the balloon wide. As she watched, the envelope began to tilt upward.

Domingo carried on pointing out things to Jose. Her brother looked as if he was in heaven. Abrienda studied Domingo. He showed no impatience with the teenager. In fact, she thought it was a great kindness he let Jose even be there, much less try the burners.

Glancing around, she didn't see anyone looking like the picture she'd seen of Teresa Valquez. Hadn't she arrived yet? There was still time, as the balloon was only half-inflated. But Abrienda would think the woman would have been there first thing.

Abrienda wondered what it would be like to be Domingo's girlfriend. She suspected he was lavish in his gifts when first squiring someone around. Did he send flowers, chocolates, gifts of jewelry?

She'd love to be wined and dined as he did it—always the best places in town. The theater, opera, sailing—all gave the women in his life a wonderful glimpse into his world. Those relationships always ended, but until they did, Abrienda thought it must be magical.

Feeling awkward and in the way, Abrienda stayed to one side, watching the activity going on around her. As the balloon rose, the basket was gradually tipped up until it sat square on the ground, the fire now shooting up into the envelope that soared overhead. The flame looked to be twice as long as Abrienda was tall. Jose and Domingo stood in the basket. It wasn't that large—four or five people might be able to travel in it—if they stood. The sides were high, made entirely of wicker. How safe was that?

The balloon looked fully inflated to her when Teresa sauntered into the area. One of the chase crew replaced Domingo in the basket and he walked toward his passenger. She was wearing high heels.

Abrienda wondered what Domingo would do. Anyone would know high heels were not suitable for a wicker basket. The skintight pants and open top looked stylish and more suitable for a walk along the beach than the early-morning chill.

As Domingo realized what the other woman wore, he took a second look. Abrienda laughed at his stunned expression.

He swung around and narrowed his gaze on her. She shrugged her shoulders and looked back at his girlfriend.

A second later he stormed over to Teresa, his hands on his hips.

"What the heck are you made up as?" he asked.

Teresa was made of sterner stuff than Abrienda expected. She merely smiled and trailed one finger down his cheek.

"I'm ready for our ride. Your assistant told me to dress warmly and in layers. This top comes off."

The men in the crew stopped their work and stared. Abrienda noticed several men from other balloons were watching, as well. Teresa didn't seem to care.

"It should, it's hardly there to begin with. What were you thinking? It's cold at the higher elevations. We'll be going up a couple of thousand feet or more," Domingo snarled.

"You can keep me warm."

He turned away in disgust. "I don't have time for this.

Julio, give me your jacket."

The slender young man on the chase crew shrugged out of his jacket and tossed it to Domingo. He in turn threw it to Teresa, who barely caught it in her surprise.

"Put that on and find some suitable shoes. We will be lifting off in less than twenty minutes. I'm not missing my time slot for you."

Domingo stormed off, leaving Teresa looking after him with a suddenly angry expression.

Jose came over to Abrienda.

"Wow, did you see? I got to fire up the burners. That was awesome. I want to go up in one of them someday."

He looked at Teresa, still standing with the jacket in her hand, glaring after Domingo. "Do you believe that woman? She's supposed to go with Dom today, but if I were him, I'd find someone else."

"*Dom?*" Abrienda echoed in surprise.

"He said I could call him that. It's what the men on the crew call him. Come on, let's go find your boss's balloon. I want to compare the two. If Mr. Alvarez can give me the specs, I might be able to calculate who really has the better chance of more distance given the wind velocity and direction. If I factor in the air volume and guesstimate the weight each would be carrying, with passengers and propane canisters and…"

He continued talking but Abrienda had lost the thread. She looked back once, wondering how the situation was going to play out. Teresa had shrugged into Julio's jacket, but she had made no move to find other shoes.

Vincente Alvarez's balloon was fully inflated and

straining the ropes that held it to the earth. Her boss and his wife were sharing a cup of coffee. Helena must be the woman standing with them. Abrienda crossed over to greet them.

"Have you met Helena yet?" her boss asked.

"Only on the phone. Nice to meet you in person," Abrienda said, noting the practical attire the woman wore. Her salt-and-pepper hair was tied back. Her fleece jacket covered a warm shirt. The jeans and rubber-soled shoes would be perfect for the flight.

Abrienda almost told Vincente about Teresa, but thought it'd go to his head. He must know her. Surely the Alvarezs went to the same functions as Ortego. She suspected Teresa would prove a lot more distraction than even Vincente had hoped for—not all in a positive manner.

"Exciting, isn't it?" Marguerite Alvarez said. She also was dressed warmly. Her hair was blowing in the breeze, but she didn't care.

Jose greeted everyone, then went to the gondola and began talking with one of the men.

"We lift off in ten," Vincente said, checking his watch once more.

"Last chance for a pit stop for a few hours. I'd better take advantage."

Helena agreed and both hurried away.

"Do you usually go with him?" Abrienda asked Mrs. Alvarez.

"Often, not always. There are always friends who like the flights. He hasn't taken you yet. After the festival, maybe he can give you and your brother a ride. Jose looks enthralled—I hope he doesn't get bitten by the bug."

Abrienda smiled and said nothing. She couldn't imagine anything compelling enough to have her get in one of those things. And they could never in a million years afford a hot air balloon, even if Jose did become smitten.

When Vincente and Helena returned, they went straight to the basket and climbed in using the step halfway up the wicker side. Testing the burners once, Vincente gave the thumbs-up to his ground crew.

A cheer was heard from the beginning of the row. Abrienda turned and saw the first balloon slowly ascend. Two minutes later the next in line began to rise. In no time she saw the black-and-red one belonging to Domingo rise. Moments later the official walked to their site and gave the release order. Slowly Vincente's balloon began moving upward.

Jose came over.

"I calculate the chances are even. The balloons are matched in size and weight carried. Though Domingo has one extra canister, Vincente is heavier than he is and has more stuff on the side pockets."

"So the race will depend on the pilot's skill," Abrienda said.

"Yeah, and if he has a competent helper—but I think Dom got shafted with that woman." Jose shook his head. "Why didn't he get someone else?"

"It was part of the bet."

She didn't tell her brother she'd been first choice. Or that Domingo had offered to donate the money to charity if he won.

Jose would love to crew for one of the balloons. And love to go up in one. Maybe she'd ask her boss if there was a place for him with the chase crew at the next outing. She wasn't as complacent about asking for a ride for her brother. What if Jose fell out?

"I'm returning home. Can I give you two a lift?" Mrs. Alvarez said.

"You're not staying?"

"The second wave will begin soon, then the third. Once all the balloons are gone, this is just an empty field. There'll be more fun at the end. But that won't be for a couple of hours, so I'll go home and await the chase team's call."

Abrienda accepted. It was much easier getting home by car than bus. Walking back to the parking lot, she looked at the balloons, the black-and-red one standing out against the more colorful ones drifting away.

She wished she could at least hear how Domingo was coping with his passenger. She grinned at the thought of what was going on. She almost felt sorry for the man.

Chapter Four

The rest of the weekend, Abrienda was kept up to speed on how the races were going by Jose's involvement. He scoured every web site and local newspaper for updates on the events and reported every fact at dinner each night.

Vincente was ahead the first two days in two drop events. Domingo surged ahead on the third day. Had Domingo been able to do all he wanted with his teammate? Or had Vincente suspected it wouldn't work out and deliberately chosen her? Would Domingo do better if he had competent help?

Abrienda thought that perhaps she could be doing Teresa a disservice. Maybe she'd caught on instantly and was of immense help. After all, she was dating Domingo, surely she'd want to do all she could to help him win.

Abrienda didn't expect her boss back in the office for more than a week. Once the festival ended on Tuesday, he and Domingo would begin the long jump to see who could go farther in their own private race. It was quiet at the office, and she relished the lack of distractions to get caught up on non priority tasks.

On Tuesday afternoon Abrienda got a call at work from Domingo Ortego.

Without any greeting, he spoke in clipped words.

"You have to fly with me starting in the morning. We leave at dawn. Pack light and for heaven's sake bring *sensible* clothes."

"What are you talking about?" Abrienda squeaked.

"The bet, what else? The festival ended at noon today. Alvarez and I are almost equal in points. The rest will be decided on the long jump."

"I'm not going. You have your teammate," she protested.

"It's you or Teresa, and she's made it clear she won't step foot inside the basket again. I'm not forfeiting this bet because of some collusion between you and Alvarez. You're the other candidate Alvarez allowed me, so I say you will come. Be here no later than five-thirty. Your bag goes with the chase team and you come with me."

"No," Abrienda exclaimed.

"I'm in no mood to argue. Be there." He hung up before she could respond.

She quickly called her boss's cell phone. He answered on the second ring.

"Abrienda, is there an emergency? Have Benito handle anything that comes up."

"Domingo Ortego just called and said I have to go with him for the next stage because Teresa won't. I can't go, Vincente. I have Jose to think about and work to do here and—" She hated to harp on her fear of heights, because that would make her seem foolish. But it was real.

Vincente laughed. "Whoa, that's better than I thought. I may win after all. Either you go or he has no assistant in the basket. Automatic forfeiture. Man, I can't wait to have him give me that check at the BBA."

"Find someone else to pair him up with."

"Hey, I did. Teresa Valquez. If she can't stay the course he's out of luck. He had two choices, and I only got one. He can't complain."

"Just so you know, I'm *not* going."

"If you say no, so be it. It's good news for me."

He rang off, leaving Abrienda feeling odd. He didn't care how he won, as long as he did. It seemed unfair that if Teresa refused to go, Domingo would have to forfeit the race—and the money for a charity of her choice.

Abrienda felt restless all evening. Even Jose picked up on her fidgeting and challenged her to a video game. She agreed, mostly to take her mind off Domingo's reaction tomorrow when she didn't show up in time for the liftoff. He'd be furious. She shivered. Still, what could he do to her? She didn't work for him.

It wasn't her fault. She'd never agreed to the stupid plan her boss had devised. Domingo couldn't expect a stranger to drop everything to accompany him. She had her own responsibilities.

Still, it was hard to fall asleep. Finally dropping off, she felt she slept for ten minutes before there was a banging on the front door to the flat.

She sprang out of bed and raced down the hall, almost colliding with her brother when he came from his room, both scrambling to don robes.

"Is it a fire?" he asked, following her to the door.

"I don't know. Maybe a neighbor needs help."

Throwing open the door, Abrienda stared in astonishment at Domingo Ortego. He appeared to loom over her, dressed in the black-and-red jumpsuit, his hair tousled and his eyes flashing.

"You're not dressed and, I expect, not packed. The shuttle buses stopped running now that the festival is over. I came to get you."

Jose greeted Domingo as if his awakening them in the middle of the night was a normal occurrence.

"I told you I'm not going," Abrienda reiterated stubbornly.

"Going where?" her brother asked.

"Ballooning—on the long jump," Domingo said. "And yes you are. I'm not losing this race on a technicality. Get your stuff."

"Wow, how cool. You get to go with Dom in the hot air balloon?" Jose said, turning a beaming face to Abrienda. "You're so lucky."

"I'm. Not. Going," she repeated slowly.

Were they both deaf?

"Abrienda, you have to. What a great chance this is. Tell me all about it when you get back. How many people get this chance? You have to go."

Jose was clearly excited. Why couldn't he be the one to go, instead of her? Perhaps she could suggest that to her boss?

"Yes she does have to go. If you convince her, I'll give you a ride when we get back," Domingo said, checking his watch. "You have ten minutes before we leave. Unless you want to travel the next few days in your pajamas, you'd better get going."

Abrienda studied his implacable expression for ten seconds, then turned and walked back to her room. She was *not* going.

Slamming the door behind her, she switched on her light and sat hard on the edge of her bed. If her boss and Domingo Ortego thought she could be ordered about to fit into their feud, they were wrong.

"I can't leave Jose," she yelled.

She could hear the two of them talking in the living room. Didn't her brother think it totally crazy that a man would show up in the middle of the night to abduct his sister? She looked at her clock. It was almost five. Domingo had better get to the launch site or he'd miss takeoff himself.

She crossed her arms over her chest. Dare she go back to bed with him still in the flat? Not that she could sleep. Her blood pounded. Her heart raced. For one insane moment she actually considered going off for a week with Domingo Ortego. Ha.

It was likely, if she didn't die of fright on ascension, she'd deck him the first chance she got. She was amazed Teresa had lasted all four days without injuring him.

Jose knocked on her door.

"I brought you one of my duffel bags and a backpack," he said. "And I can manage myself while you're gone. I'm almost eighteen. Besides, Dom said he'd have his housekeeper come to cook my meals. How cool is that."

"I can cook your meals," she said, annoyed Domingo seemed to think he could get everyone to jump to his commands by a snap of his fingers.

The door banged open and Domingo stood in the opening, seeming to fill the space. Jose stood beside him. Both looked at Abrienda.

"I'm serious. If you don't come willingly, I'll bring you however I can. You will be on that balloon for the next seven days," Domingo said levelly.

She glared at him. "I'm afraid of heights."

"Oh, yeah, I forgot about that," Jose said.

"So sit in the bottom of the basket and keep your eyes shut. You now have five minutes left until we leave."

Abrienda fumed as she sat in the passenger seat of the sports car. Domingo ignored her as he quickly sped through the almost empty streets. She wasn't at all happy—with either Domingo or Jose. Why did men band together whenever it suited them? She'd expected better of her brother.

"There'll be coffee and food at the launch site. I don't want to stop before that," he said at one point.

She ignored him. Hunger was the least of her worries. The closer they drew to the field, the more anxious she became. He couldn't be seriously planning on her joining him.

Of course he was. She wouldn't be in the car if he weren't.

"What happened to your girlfriend?" she asked, surreptitiously wiping her palms against her pants.

Her fear increased. She couldn't go up in a balloon. For heaven's sake, she had trouble going above the fifth floor in high-rise buildings. And there she was encased in glass and steel.

Yet Domingo and Jose expected her to dangle from a large balloon in a flimsy wicker basket high above the earth? She couldn't do it.

She glanced at him when he didn't answer right away and saw the anger simmering. With a flick of his eyes her way, he replied, "She wanted a golden band on her finger. That was not in the cards, so she bailed. Good riddance, I say. She complained more than anyone I know. I need someone I can count on. If she's that unreliable, what would happen if she ditched me halfway through? At least this way, I was able to get you."

He glanced at her. "You don't have to do anything but go along for the ride. A lot of people would love the opportunity."

Abrienda cleared her throat.

"Truly. I really am very afraid of heights. I'm likely to faint or throw up or something that would impede your flight. You have to explain that to Vincente and get someone else."

"If you faint, do it in a corner so you won't be in my way. If you throw up, do it over the side. I can think of nothing Alvarez would love better than for me to have no one to accompany me. Instant forfeit."

She stared at him. He couldn't be so coldhearted as to ignore a truly serious phobia!

"It's just a stupid bet," she muttered rebelliously.

"You wouldn't say that if it was *your* reputation and money on the line," he returned.

"I wouldn't have made the bet in the first place."

A flicker of amusement flashed on his face, replaced almost immediately by the fierce concentration she was growing to know.

"I bet there a lot of things I do that you wouldn't," he said.

A short time later Domingo turned into the road that led to the field. Dawn was just a lightening of the sky in the east. The sun wouldn't rise for another half hour or so.

Abrienda looked at the startling difference from when she was here before. There were only two balloons, both glowing from their burners in the darkened sky. As they were almost fully inflated, she knew she didn't have much time to convince this man she really couldn't go.

"You should have taken Jose," she said, staring in horror at the gleaming red-and-black balloon.

"Terms from your boss were clear. You're my fall-back choice. Though, if you'd just accepted in the first place, you'd already have four days of experience."

"I'll just hold you up."

She was desperate. What could she say to convince him?

He stopped the car next to a small truck and two other cars. Turning to face her, he reached out and caught her chin, turning her face to his.

"Sabotage this race and you'll regret it."

She pulled away and glared at him.

"I was insulted the first time you suggested such a thing. I don't need to sabotage anything. But I don't have to help. That'll be enough detriment to let my boss win."

"I doubt it. The balloon only needs one pilot. I'm it. Let's go."

She sat in the car when he got out, wondering if she could open her door and run down the road to escape. No, almost certainly he'd just follow and pull her back again. As she stared at the balloon, her heart pumped like a piston.

He opened her door and unfastened her seat belt. She slapped his hands away.

"I'm not some child," she said, getting out and judging the chances of her getting away in the darkness, which was quickly fading into daylight. Not good.

He took her hand and walked toward the group of people working around the balloon. Did he suspect her thoughts?

Two men near the balloon saw them and called a greeting. The rest turned and also called out.

"I wasn't sure you'd make it back in time," one man said.

"Her case is in the back of the car. Get it. Abrienda, this is Manuel. That's Julio and Maria and Paolo. Paolo is your boss's man. Abrienda will take Teresa's place. Maria, do you have a jacket she can wear?"

She knew he suspected her frantic plan to escape when he didn't release her. In only a moment Maria returned with a black jacket slashed by the red band. Domingo handed it to Abrienda, releasing her at last.

"Put it on, it'll be cooler the higher we go. You can take it off later when it grows warm."

Vincente Alvarez came into the light.

"Want to call it off?" he asked Domingo, grinning maliciously.

"No need, I have my passenger," Domingo said, nodding to Abrienda.

Vincente turned and saw her.

"Oh, you're kidding. Abrienda?" He laughed.

The tone made her look at him.

"What does that mean?" she asked angrily.

"Nothing, Abrienda. Only that it's in the bag now." He lifted his hand in a half wave and turned to walk back to his own balloon. "Liftoff in fifteen minutes," he called back.

Maria walked to the gondola, carrying a couple of soda cans and a small bag. Leaning over the side, she handed them in to Manuel, who was operating the burners. He stowed them in small pouches affixed to the side of the basket.

"You have two blankets in the large bag, water, snacks, and Julio double-checked the fuel supply, so you're good to go."

She frowned at Abrienda.

"You don't look ready. Last chance for a toilet break for the next few hours. Come on, I'll show you the loo."

Abrienda protested, but there was no help for it. Whether she liked it or not, and she did so *not*, it looked as if she was going up in a hot air balloon.

Fourteen minutes later Abrienda placed her foot in the small step built into the side of the gondola and scrambled over into the basket feeling as if she would be physically sick. If she'd had anything to eat, she knew it would have come right back up.

The basket sat on solid ground, it didn't move, but the loud noise of the burners and the ringing shouts of the ground crew fed her nervousness. A second later Domingo jumped in, exchanging places with Manuel. When Manuel climbed out of the gondola, they were ready to go.

"Keep up," he shouted as he fed the fire, and the flames leaped high into the large balloon overhead.

Abrienda cringed and looked for a corner to sit in. The basket was not exactly spacious, and valuable space was taken up with large propane tanks, all connected to interconnecting hoses that fed the burners.

She backed to an area against the side next to one of the tanks and sat down. Keeping her knees bent, she stayed out of Domingo's way.

"There're blankets in that side pouch if you want to sit on them," he said, pointing to a flap covering a canvas basket affixed to the side. She pulled both out. Neither was large, but at least it beat sitting directly on the wicker. Wedging her back against the corner made by the basket and tank, she closed her eyes. When the basket lurched, she gripped the edge of the blankets and began praying. She knew her last moments on earth were about to end.

Another lurch, the burners roaring, and suddenly the sounds of voices faded. She could only hear the burners. Two minutes later there was silence.

Slowly she opened her eyes. Domingo stared down at her.

"You weren't kidding about being afraid of heights, were you?" he asked.

He had one hand on the control knob of the burners, but they were not shooting flame up into the balloon. There was only silence. The basket was slowly swaying, almost like floating in a pool. Or a cloud.

She unclenched her hands, flexing her stiff fingers. It was cool up here, but not unpleasantly so. The sky around her was growing lighter.

"We're floating?" she asked.

"Yes. If you're serious about getting sick, stay where you are. I don't want that."

Then he opened the burners and a roar sounded as loud as a motorcycle as the flames leaped. Five seconds later he shut off the burners again.

Silence.

For a long moment Abrienda sat where she was. She stretched her legs out in front of her. Domingo was less than six inches away. Glancing around she noted how cramped the basket seemed. Due, no doubt, to the large propane tanks. Several people could ride as long as they stood, as there was space at each side of the basket. Storage pouches lined the walls. The tubes from the tanks were tucked under the covering at the top edge of the basket. Looking up, she saw the burners above Domingo's head, still a good distance from the huge balloon that filled her sight.

Curiosity flickered. "How high up are we?" she asked.

He looked over the edge of the basket and her heart skipped a beat. What if he fell out? She'd be alone in the sky. She caught her breath.

"Don't do that!" she said sharply.

"Do what?" he asked.

"Lean over the edge like that. What if you fall out?"

He laughed, looking around and then up at the balloon.

"I'm not going to fall out. I'd have to climb up on the side to do so. But you'd feel better if you know how to operate the balloon. Come and I'll show you."

"I'm not moving," she vowed.

He was right, it was unlikely anyone would fall out. The high sides were almost chest high for her. Still, freak accidents could happen.

"You're missing a great sight, Barcelona from the air. No truck or car noises. No pollution. Only the beauty of the city as it wakens against the blue of the Med. You may never have this opportunity again."

She definitely would not do this again. She was tempted to peek. But the thought of looking down from so high caused a wave of nausea to sweep over her. She dropped her gaze to

Domingo's feet. She could do this as long as she didn't move. She drew a deep, slow breath.

The basket swayed and she grabbed the edge of the blankets. Looking up, she saw Domingo right over her.

"Get back in the middle, you'll dump us both out!" she yelled.

"It'll never happen. Really, come see this view. You'll regret it forever if you don't."

"I can't."

"Stretch yourself, you'll be amazed what you can do if you just try."

He almost lifted her to her feet by his grip on one arm. Once standing, she pressed closer to him, her theory being he'd done this before and was less likely to fall than she was.

"Look."

He stretched out his right hand, his left still holding on to her. "See Alvarez's balloon? It's lower than ours, he's following a different air current. Still going pretty much the same direction, but not moving as fast as we are."

Slowly she moved her gaze across the edge of the basket and looked. She could see her boss's balloon, not too far distant, but definitely lower. She swallowed hard. How high were they?

"Now, look over there, you see the Serra de Collserola?" he asked, pointing to the high ridge that enclosed Barcelona on the northwest. "Beautiful."

She jumped a second later when he casually reached up and depressed the lever to the burners. Flame shot up. A few seconds later he glanced at one of the gauges near the burners and released the lever.

Silence once again. Peaceful and amazing.

The sun had risen enough to illuminate the top edge of the ridge. Slowly the light moved down the slopes and toward the city. Abrienda watched, moving her gaze slowly down until she saw some of the spires and buildings lighted by the rising sun.

Forgetting her fear of heights, she leaned against Domingo's solid strength and watched mesmerized as the city she'd lived in all her life was wakened with light from the sun. The white buildings began to gleam in the early light. Windows looked as if they were on fire as they reflected the early rays. She could see the grid pattern of the streets and the large yachts and boats in the harbor.

It was breathtaking.

She looked around, still feeling as if any movement beyond her eyes would plunge her over the side and several thousand feet to the earth below. But she couldn't resist. The sea was a dark blue, stretching to the curvature of the earth.

It was hard to tell in which direction they were traveling. In fact, there was no sensation of movement at all except for the gentle swaying of the basket.

Chapter Five

"Are we still rising?" she asked.

"We've leveled off a bit. I'll need to heat the air soon to stay with this current."

"But we're moving?"

"Sure. When the sun's higher, you can watch our shadow move across the land, judge how fast we're traveling."

"How fast?"

"Depends on the air current. We're just along for the ride."

He let her go and depressed the burner lever again. The roar of the flame startled her. She was afraid to move a fraction. She had her balance, but could she drop to the floor and crawl back to her corner without making the basket tip?

"Relax, Abrienda, you won't fall out."

His voice was warm, right beside her ear.

"Don't we have to balance the weight or something?" she asked, slowly turning to face him.

He was so close she blinked. Granted, the basket wasn't that large, but he didn't need to be so close. She felt her nerves tighten with an emotion other than fear.

"The ropes holding the basket to the balloon are evenly spaced. They support the weight. Even if we are both on one side, the basket isn't going to tip."

She nodded, trying to calm her nerves with the rational tone of his voice. Trying to ignore the attraction that flared and remember she was on this ride under protest.

She could do this. She had to, what choice did she have?

Slowly taking a deep breath, she looked out again. She might as well savor every experience to tell Jose. He'd certainly pepper her with questions the next time he talked to her.

There was no feeling of movement, but the competing balloon seemed to drop away. Abrienda knew they had to be rising, but she had nothing to gauge their height. Not as high as an airplane, she knew that. But higher than she'd ever been.

She looked at Domingo. He was studying her.

"Shouldn't you be watching where we're going? What if we crash into a plane or something?"

"I hope that won't happen," he said easily. "Want a turn with the burners?"

He shut them down and the silence again enveloped them.

"It's weird. One moment I can hardly think because of the noise, then there's that blissful silence."

"Combined with the floating sensation, it's a high, isn't it?" he added. "That's why I love it. Silently drifting over the earth, seeing things from a new perspective."

She shrugged. She was glad the experience wasn't turning out to be as bad as she'd anticipated. No thanks to the man who had practically forced her out of her home and into this flimsy wicker basket.

"Come." He reached out his hand. She took it and let him pull her even closer. With his firm grip she felt safe. How odd was that? She didn't even like the man. He practically kidnapped her and put her in mortal danger.

Yet who else was she going to trust at this moment? She wasn't sure her boss warranted her trust anymore. How dare he make her a condition of the bet.

Once she stood next to Domingo, she could smell the unique scent that was his. She wanted to close her eyes and savor the tangy aroma. It was totally masculine and had her heart beating faster.

The other problem—staying immune to this man for a week. Now, *that* she wasn't sure she was capable of doing.

"I'll explain," he said.

She loved his voice from the first moment she'd heard it. Now she watched as his lips moved forming the sounds that produced speech. She savored how deep and melodious it sounded, the smooth way he pronounced his words, how the resonance gave her goose bumps along her skin. If she closed her eyes, would he continue talking?

"Got it?" he asked.

"No." She blinked.

She'd been enjoying the sound, not paying attention to the explanation.

He lifted her hand and placed it on the grip. The burners themselves were above passengers. No fire danger, at least, or bumping heads by walking into them.

"Now," he said, letting go.

She pulled and let go immediately when the roar of the fire startled her.

He reached out and grabbed the grip with one hand, pulling her hand back with the other.

"Try again," he said.

There was no censure in his tone, which surprised her. She'd have thought him too impatient to let such a blunder pass without a scathing complaint.

She gripped hard and pulled steadily until she felt the grip stop, holding on while the flames soared into the balloon, the roar almost deafening.

"Won't it catch fire?" she asked, venturing a look up at the huge canopy above them. The opening was a wide circle. She couldn't judge how high the top was, but it looked a long way up. The fire rose ten feet or so, yet didn't come close to the balloon material.

"Check the gauge there." He pointed. "That tells us the temperature at the top. Let go."

The burners went silent.

"I keep it around that temperature. When it drops we fire up again. We stop the flame when it gets there. The material surrounding the opening is fire retardant and the flame is far enough away not to ignite. Of course, the rest of the balloon is too far from the flame to burn, either, as long as we don't get it too hot inside."

She gazed up into the balloon for a moment, then looked at him. His dark eyes watched her, narrowed as if in speculation.

For a fleeting second, Abrienda wished she were a beautiful blonde with the figure of a model. Would he want to take her places, spend time with her?

Feeling foolish, she looked away as reason returned. She didn't have what it took to captivate a man like Domingo Ortego. He was used to the most beautiful women in Europe. Women who weren't afraid of heights, or who owned more than one basic black cocktail dress to wear to office parties. Women who knew what to say to him when stranded in a basket hundreds of feet in the air.

"Better?" he asked.

She nodded. Bravely she looked around. Then down. Not being near the edge, she could only see the earth at a distance. Like from the lookout point at the top of the Collserola. She could do this. For a moment she felt giddy with relief.

"How far will we travel today?" she asked.

"I have no idea. That's what makes it an adventure. The wind is the sole factor in determining that. Currently we are moving about fifteen miles an hour."

"And when we land?"

"Actually, we'll sail until we run low on fuel. Then we hope to find a field large enough to hold the balloon when it's deflated."

"What if crops are growing in the field? Or it has cattle or something?"

"We hope they'll still accommodate the balloon. We communicate with the chase team from here." He pointed to a handheld radio on top of the cooler. "They move a lot faster than we do. If we locate a place, they'll negotiate with the owners when we think we'll be setting down. Except to flatten things temporarily, there is no lasting damage."

"Can the chase team keep up?" she asked.

"They always have," he replied. "We aren't moving as fast as they are, so even though the roads won't necessarily go the same direction we're going, they'll have plenty of time to circle round and be waiting when we come down."

"So we don't know where we're going. Don't know where

we're spending the night. Don't know what we'll have for dinner," she murmured.

It sounded awfully unsettling.

"Pretty much," he said.

Firing up the burners again, he turned his attention to altitude and wind direction.

Abrienda grew brave enough to approach the side of the basket on her own. Reaching out, she grabbed on to the top and, staying an arm's distance away, looked around. As long as she didn't look down, she thought she'd be okay. It actually was tolerable. She knew Jose would love it. Would she get used to it by the end of the week? Would she even grow to enjoy it, perhaps?

Vincente Alvarez's balloon was rising. Soon it was as high as theirs, though still some distance away. She could barely make out Vincente and Helena. The other woman waved and Abrienda lifted her hand in return.

She turned, still holding on to the edge with one hand.

"How did you get into hot air ballooning? I'd think you'd prefer race cars or flying airplanes or something," she asked Domingo.

"This is more subtle. Pitting skill and knowledge of topography and air currents and thermal patterns to find the level that offers the best speed and in a direction I wish to go. Auto racing is fun, but once I've mastered a track, it's becomes merely a question of speed."

"But in this, don't you go where the air blows? There's no control."

"There is. There are different air currents at different levels, light nuances if you like. Finding the right level is what makes it challenging. Balloons are maneuverable to a certain extent if you know where the air is blowing."

"And, of course, the biggest challenge is winning," she said.

"There is that," he replied.

When he shut down the burners, he picked up the radio mike and called the chase crew.

They had the balloon in sight, Manuel reported. They were almost directly beneath them but the road veered in the opposite direction soon according to their map, so they might have to find an alternate route. If it looked as if Domingo would drift out of range, they'd let him know.

Abrienda looked over the side to see if she could find the chase vehicle and felt a wave of nausea overtake her. She closed her eyes and sank to her knees. Heart pounding, she thought she'd be sick. Slowly drawing in deep breaths, she tried to quell the sensation. No more of that. She'd had a false sense of security, but one look at how far down the ground was and she felt scared to death.

Taking a couple more deep breaths helped, then she scooted over to the corner with the blankets and sat on them again. She hated this feeling. And she hated that she acted like this in front of Domingo Ortego. He feared nothing. How silly she must seem.

Domingo finished talking and then took a bottle of water from one of the storage pouches.

"Want something?" he asked.

Abrienda shook her head. If he hadn't burst into her apartment and practically forced her on this stupid trip, she'd be having a nice breakfast with Jose instead of being terrified out of her wits, cold, and uncomfortable sitting on the floor of a flimsy basket dangling from a balloon by only a few thin ropes. What if one broke?

She glared at Domingo, wondering how anyone found this fun. He was clearly enjoying himself. His dark hair was tousled, unlike the sleek look when he was at work. He had unzipped his jacket and it revealed a tight black T-shirt beneath, lovingly sculpting his muscular chest. Tantalized, she stared, wondering what he'd look like wearing only a bathing suit or nothing at all.

Shocked at her thoughts, she looked away, but not far in the small basket. And if she looked up, it would be to see Domingo or the balloon overhead.

Endless minutes passed as slowly as any Abrienda had lived through. For the most part Domingo ignored her. She didn't care. She wasn't one of his friends. She wanted to get on the ground and never leave it again. She drew her knees up and wrapped her arms around her legs. She was getting used to the cool air, feeling it gradually warm as the sun rose higher.

When Domingo switched the valve on the propane tanks, she watched. There were six large tanks taking up most of room in the basket. How far would they get on those tanks? She surmised the chase team had extras to swap out when they landed.

Could she hitch a ride back with them?

Only if she could convince Domingo that she couldn't go on. Or maybe it was Vincente she had to convince. She'd ask her boss to let Domingo find someone else to continue the race. She wanted to go home.

"What happens when we run out of gas?" she asked.

There would be no midair refueling.

"We'll put down. When we reach halfway on the last tank, we'll start looking for a landing site. I don't want to run totally out of propane, it's what keeps us maneuverable."

"Up and down, maybe, but not in any other direction."

"That's enough to get us where we want. The closer to earth, the more we'll rely on reading the wind from the plants and trees on the ground."

Dom looked at Abrienda and almost felt sorry for her. She wasn't having the time of her life. Too bad her boss had made her a part of the bet. Or too bad Teresa got greedy and wanted more than the good times they'd enjoyed together.

Her ultimatum had been unexpected. He thought she enjoyed what they had as much as he did. But the lure of riches and a lasting place in Barcelona society proved too much. Demanding he commit to more than he wanted had been the last straw. She'd left yesterday in a huff and he didn't expect to see her again anytime soon. He certainly wasn't going to ask her to marry him.

He himself didn't hold much stock in marriage—not with his own parents as examples.

Financially, his father and grandfather had made a lot of money for the family. He was doing as well with his own company. But he wasn't some royal who had to ensure continuation of the family.

He had a brother who was married and already had two children. He and his wife were talking about a third. Those grandchildren would satisfy any errant grandparent genes his parents might discover at some future date.

He was content to do what he wanted, when he wanted—

without some wife in the background.

Teresa had seemed to enjoy the ballooning at the festival. At least she hadn't huddled in a corner, looking white and scared. How could anyone not love the freedom rising above the earth brought? He flew airplanes, with a different feeling. This was quiet, peaceful and beautiful. Slow and leisurely. The views were amazing. The sense of tranquility an unexpected bonus.

They were drifting over the countryside north and a bit west of Barcelona. The winds from the Med would continue in this direction for another month before shifting. He enjoyed watching the mountainous terrain, with the tree-covered valleys and canyons.

Here and there a road wound through the open land.

A reservoir sparkled in the sunshine. A small village opened in another valley.

He studied the earth as if it was a living map. He knew the chase car would have a hard time following if the balloon continued in the mountainous terrain. Could he get over this range before having to set down?

He carried more fuel than usual, but he wasn't going to risk the safety of the balloon or his passenger by pushing to the extreme limit. He was determined to win the bet, but not if it put Abrienda in real danger.

If Manuel or Maria had been his crew, they'd have plenty to talk about. The silence when the burners were off was beginning to wear on his nerves. Abrienda could at least talk to him while sitting where she was with her eyes closed.

"How old is your brother?" he asked at the next quiet time.

"He'll be eighteen soon."

"So, still in school? How is it he lives with you? Are your parents divorced?"

"No, they died."

"I'm sorry."

She shrugged. "It was nine years ago. Jose was only eight when they died."

"You couldn't have been that much older yourself."

She flashed him a look.

"I was nineteen. I had just started university."

"So you had to care for him—there were no other relatives to help?"

She shook her head.

"Future plans?"

She leaned back against the side of the basket to look up at him.

"He's going to university," she said with pride. "He plans to study physics. I think that's why he was so interested in the how-to of flying this thing. He should be here, not me. He'd love it."

"I can see Vincente's rationale in having you partner me. If he knew me better, he'd know I'll put up with almost anything to win. I'm sorry you aren't enjoying the ride. But blame him, not me," Domingo returned.

"Does that mean Teresa was a big help?"

She was annoyed that even that society woman had outperformed her. At least Abrienda felt she'd dressed more appropriately.

"Different situation, but she helped more than you're doing."

"So what do you need me for? You know how to fly this thing. I'd only be in the way."

"You could talk to me to make the time go faster."

"You want to hear about the exciting life of a personal assistant to a busy businessman? Somehow I doubt it."

"Why not? It'll be a novelty."

He liked the flash of fire she displayed from time to time.

He knew his cavalier attitude rubbed her the wrong way. He should stop, but he was intrigued by the bursts of emotions that were quickly damped down. What would she be like if she let herself go with no restraints?

In a monotone she recited, "We get up and eat. I go to work, Jose to school. I come home and prepare dinner and we eat. He studies, I clean, do laundry or shopping. We go to sleep. How's that for excitement?"

"You don't mention a special friend."

She shrugged. "Now is not the time to be dating. I have my brother to raise."

"What happened to your parents?"

"They died in a boating accident."

From what he could guess, money was an issue. Apparently the parents had not left their offspring comfortably covered in the financial realm.

"What would you do if you could do anything you wanted?" he asked.

She didn't hesitate. "Be a website designer. I would love to study graphic design, learn more about all the aspects of website design and work from home on projects that I selected. Working hours I choose."

He nodded slowly. He'd heard somewhere that a

secretary's job was very stressful because they had so little control over it. They were at the beck and call of the boss they worked for.

He glanced across to the other balloon, still some distance away. He couldn't see Helena clearly but wondered what she'd do if she could do anything she wanted. He'd never asked. It probably wouldn't be to support all his endeavors.

The balloon spun around and began to waffle. Domingo quickly assessed the situation. There was an eddy of wind causing problems. Glancing around, he saw the other balloon also turning. Quickly opening the valve of the burners, he tried to rise above the turbulent air. Slowly the wild gyrations ceased.

Abrienda had her eyes tightly closed and her hands clenched into fists, arms wrapped around her up bent legs.

"Are we going to crash?" she asked in a tight voice.

Chapter Six

"Not today," Domingo replied.

The balloon stabilized. Once the erratic motion ceased, Abrienda opened her eyes. Domingo wished she'd get over her fear and enjoy the trip. It'd make it more pleasant for her, since she was essentially stuck with a week's assignment in the air.

And easier on him as the hours stretched out.

Not that he should care. Vincente had known his PA wouldn't be an asset—while Helena was extremely efficient. She had probably mastered the controls and was offering Vincente streamlined ways to do things.

Still, it was Domingo who maintained a slight lead. If he could increase it over the next few days, he'd win the bet.

Giving another blast, he shut down the burners and went to sit beside his unwilling crew. The space was tight and his leg brushed against hers.

She shifted a couple of inches away and the action caused him to give way to the devilment that rose.

He reached for her hand, prying the fist open and interlacing his fingers with hers. She tugged, but he held on.

"Let go," she said.

"We need to get some ground rules established," he said,

ignoring her attempts to pull free. It gave him hope she really didn't want to. It was so much easier to get things he wanted if women met him halfway.

"Like what?" she asked. He could hear the reluctant curiosity in her tone.

"Like, you can't sit in this corner the entire seven days."

"I told you I have a fear of heights."

Slowly he traced the back of her hand with his thumb. Her skin was silky soft and cool.

"So don't look down. Look out. Forget the space beneath us and enjoy the beauty of the flight. Together we can win this race."

"You practically kidnapped me and now you expect me to help you?"

"I do. Make the most of the chance, as Jose said. And show your boss you don't answer to him outside of work. *He* put you in this situation, not I."

She thought it over a moment.

Domingo moved closer. He liked women, especially pretty ones with big brown eyes and windblown brown hair with streaks of gold.

"Pretend—if only for a week—that this is what you want. If we win, the money goes to your favorite charity—which you have not yet told me. If Alvarez wins, we get nothing and so all this effort will be in vain."

She studied him with those large eyes, questioning, weighing.

"Maybe."

Victory was close, he could feel it.

Leaning back, he continued to caress her hand, waiting.

Maybe he needed to make the pot sweeter.

"If we win, I'll treat you and your brother to a week at a place of your choice."

"Do you think you can *bribe* me, Señor Ortego?' she immediately said hotly. "It is enough to have the money be put to use and not just exchanged from one rich man to another."

That response was not what he'd expected.

"Do you have something against rich men?" he asked.

"Only when they are foolish in the extreme."

He smiled slowly. "Like this bet?"

"Exactly. You shouldn't have made the stupid wager."

"But I did, and here we are. He's the one who made the terms. You help me, I donate the winnings," he said.

"And if you don't win?"

"I won't even consider that. But if I lose, I'll still donate to your charity."

"It's a win-win for me then. So why would I help?" Abrienda asked.

"For honor," he said slowly.

He knew more about this woman than she suspected. He was good at judging character and knew integrity was important to her.

She watched his thumb rubbing her hand for a long moment. He wondered if she would capitulate or continue to defy him. It would prove a long week if they weren't pulling together.

"Agreed. Either way I win, but I'll do what I can to make sure we both win," she said slowly.

Tugging her hand again, she watched as he slowly released

her. Was that disappointment in her eyes?

"But you needn't try your blandishments on me," she continued. "I know you were voted Barcelona's most eligible bachelor last year, but I'm not one of your society women to date for a couple of months before moving on. This is strictly business. Agreed?"

"Most certainly not. You fascinate me, Abrienda. You don't want me to grow bored on the flight, do you?"

He loved being with her. She was so different from the other women he knew.

"I don't care much about what you do on the flight. Just win so the money goes to the Sisters of Charity Children's Home. That was my parents' favorite charity and I want you to donate in their names."

"And something for you?"

"Nothing for me."

Domingo studied her expression for a moment. She was serious. It threw his calculations off. How could she not want something for herself? Everyone did. He didn't mind, he had the money to indulge himself and his friends. He knew how life went. Those with money were targeted by those without. It wasn't good or bad, just the way things were.

Or the way he thought they were. What was Abrienda's game?

"What?" Abrienda asked.

She found his stare unnerving, as if he were trying to dissect her or something.

"Just thinking," he replied, and looked away.

For a moment she wanted to ask him about what, but thought it best to leave things alone. He had already unsettled her enough for one day. She tucked her hands against her chest, still feeling the warmth of his palm, the erotic rubbing of his thumb. She wished he'd held on a bit more.

Getting hot and bothered by his presence sure beat being afraid for her life. Though, given the two choices, she suspected that riding in the wretched balloon was safer than getting caught up with Domingo Ortego.

Yet she wouldn't be human, wouldn't be a woman if she wasn't intrigued by his sexy good looks and charming manner. She knew it had to be calculated. He'd been getting his own way for far too long to change his manner of operating.

For a few seconds she'd let herself go, imagined he really cared for her. It would be beyond anything she'd ever experienced to have a romantic relationship with Domingo.

Her heart raced at the thought and she looked away lest he catch a glimmer of the awareness that rose every time she came near him. Actually, if she were honest with herself, every time she even thought about him.

"So what are the rules?" she asked a moment later.

He looked back and smiled. The light dancing in his eyes almost had her groaning with pleasure. He looked incredibly masculine with that devil-may-care look, and incredibly sexy with that smile.

"We pull together, all for one, one for all."

She laughed. "That's original."

He smiled again. "Agreed?"

"I'm not out to sabotage your race," she repeated.

"So there's no problem with that one."

"There're more rules?"

He leaned closer. "We spend time getting to know each

other."

Her breath caught. He was close enough that she could feel his breath brush against her cheeks. Close enough that leaning forward only a few scant inches would put her mouth against his, her lips brushing his.

"We know each other quite well enough."

Was that breathless voice hers? She wanted to jump up and run away. A quick flick around the gondola convinced her that was totally impossible.

"We could know each other even better," he said, his fingers brushing her hair lightly.

She jerked back as if stung, scooting away several inches and trying to show her displeasure. Only, she was afraid her reaction was a bit extreme.

"Didn't we just agree you are wasting your time trying to charm me?" she said.

"Ah, but it's so much fun," he said, watching her with those dark eyes.

"I don't think there's any point in it."

"It will make the journey more interesting. We can become friends."

She rolled her eyes at that notion.

"Or lovers."

She snapped her gaze right back at him.

"You're crazy. We don't know each other enough to ever get to that level."

"It doesn't take long to get to know someone when confined to such a small space for endless hours," he said, his voice deliberately pitched low and sexy.

She raised her right hand, index finger shaking at him.

"Stop right there. We are *not* going to become that close."

He leaned back and stretched out his long legs, taking up all the available floor space

"Maybe not. But it's worth thinking about."

"You need to think about this balloon and keeping us up in the air," she said, scarcely able to form two words together as the mere thought of them tangled together in lovemaking almost erased all her thought processes.

He leaned over and touched her cheek lightly and then rose in one easy movement and glanced around at the gauge. A second later the jets roared to life.

Once her breathing was under control, Abrienda stood and looked around. Looking out instead of down, she spotted the other balloon. It looked closer than before. Now it was slightly higher than they were.

"Clear sailing until the ambient air warms too much to make it easy to keep our altitude," he said.

She nodded, amazed he could switch off the charm and move to dedicated racer in a heartbeat. She was still reeling from their discussion.

And wondering what it would be like to be a close, very personal, friend of Domingo's.

Domingo switched to the last fuel canister later. He was not getting as much lift as earlier when the air temperature had been cooler. Time to begin looking for a place to stop and exchange these tanks for fresh ones.

It was early afternoon. He'd already covered more distance than every day of the festival combined. The wind was steady and probably moving them more than twenty miles an hour. He estimated they'd covered more than a hundred miles.

The mountainous terrain below didn't offer many wide meadows where there would be room to set down and let the envelope deflate without becoming tangled with trees or ground growth.

The chase crew would have replacement tanks and plenty of food, as well as the tents and bedrolls he hoped they wouldn't have to use. If he didn't have to rough it, he'd choose not to.

On the other hand, dossing down on a sleeping bag beneath the stars was something he'd done more than once. Once they refueled they'd be off again. Long jumps were also an endurance event. He'd go for a few more miles before setting down for the night.

Abrienda hadn't said a word for a while. She'd gradually relaxed enough to doze for a few minutes but she hadn't offered to help in any way. So much for a truce.

If Alvarez thought that would slow him down, the man had rocks in his head.

"We'll be setting down soon," Domingo said to Julio when he'd reached the chase team on the radio. He scanned the terrain for a suitable place. "Where are you?"

"You're a bit behind us and farther north. Maria has you in our sights comparing it with the topographical map. Do you see any place to set down? How far ahead of Alvarez are you?"

Domingo noticed Abrienda was awake now and watching him.

"His balloon set down about twenty minutes ago. I'm riding at half tank on the last one right now and would prefer to come down soon. But all I see is tree-covered hills."

"Wait, Maria says there's a new reservoir north of your position. Any chance you could get near that? There should be plenty of cleared space. Just don't land in the water."

With that Abrienda rose and clutched the side of the basket, looking around.

"We aren't going to land in water, are we?"

"Can't swim?" he asked.

"Of course I can swim, but I'm not dressed for it. What if the balloon comes down on top of us and drowns us?" she asked anxiously.

"Relax, we're not landing in water. Often reservoirs have a lot of cleared land surrounding them, to allow for water fluctuation."

He spoke back into the radio, "I see a clearing, and a road leading to it. We're lined up for it, I'll try for that."

The balloon began descending.

"We're heading in that direction," Manuel said.

She looked around. "Where's the other balloon?"

"They put down already."

"Why would they do that?"

"If he found a meadow Vincente wanted to take advantage of, he'd land. He needs fuel. So do we. Once we switch out the tanks, we'll be good to go again."

"Why didn't we put down when he did?"

She'd wanted time to talk to Vincente, get him to agree to let someone else take her place. Maybe she could switch with Maria and be part of the ground crew.

He smiled at her tone.

"Don't you like to win?" he asked.

"Not if we're risking our lives!" she snapped.

"We're not. Relax. I promise to get you home all in one piece," he said.

He saw the reservoir. He wished he had a better way to gauge the wind rather than flying in it to see where he ended up.

Experience told him if they continued at the current rate, they should reach ground about the time they reached the cleared area surrounding the water.

"When we get on the ground, one of us has to keep the envelope inflated enough to keep it from tangling with the trees. The other has to jump out with a rope and secure the basket to the ground. Which task do you want?" he asked.

"Neither," she said, glancing around as if looking for a third alternative.

"I need your help in this, Abrienda," he said. "This is no time to argue. We'll be on the ground, so your phobia about height shouldn't get in the way."

She glanced up at the balloon overhead.

"I can't keep it properly inflated. I'll try to tie the rope."

"Don't try, do."

She glared at him.

"Tell me how I'm supposed to do that and I'll do my best. I am not here to sabotage your blasted race. Though if something happened, I'd sure get home sooner."

"Don't even think it."

She looked away. Her anger seemed to drive away her fear.

He gave her directions, keeping an eye on the rapidly approaching clearing. It was going to be a bit more tricky than he liked—especially with a novice on board. But unexpected challenges were what made the race interesting.

In less than ten minutes he set the basket down right at the edge of the clearing at least a dozen feet or more from the water's edge.

As soon as it hit the ground he yelled at Abrienda to jump off and grab one of the tethering ropes. She used the step in the side to scramble over the edge and he heard her land, then jump to her feet and pull on the rope.

"There's nothing here to tie it to. If you lift off, I'm letting go," she called.

He could see her over the edge of the basket. It skidded along the ground for a few feet. He glanced at the balloon. He wanted to keep it as inflated as possible for quick rising once the tanks were switched, but not so much it pulled against the basket while they were on the ground.

He didn't want to skid across the ground, but couldn't let the envelope collapse all the way or they'd take valuable minutes reinflating it.

"Wait, there's a stump sticking up. It's a big one, maybe too big for the rope to go around."

Her voice faded as she disappeared from view. He looked over the edge. She was winding the rope tightly around a stump. If she didn't secure it just right, it could slip off. Frustrated, Domingo wanted to jump off and do it himself, but it would be a stupid move to leave the balloon unmanned.

When she finished, she looked up and smiled. Standing, she did a little dance.

"I'm on the ground again," she shouted, turning in a big circle, her arms outstretched.

"Take this rope and secure a second anchor," he called,

tying another to the frame and tossing it to her.

She found another stump and quickly tied that rope then sat on the stump and looked up at the balloon, then around the clearing. The basket was anchored. Now it was up to the chase crew to find them.

Domingo tried the radio again, but being lower than the surrounding hills, the signal wasn't reaching the rest of the team.

There was nothing to do but wait.

"How long do you need to keep the balloon inflated?" she called.

"Until the crew can switch out the empty tanks with full ones, or we run out of propane. If that happens, I'll need your help to keep the balloon away from the water and the trees."

"How long before they get here?"

"Whenever they get here."

Abrienda went to the water's edge and gazed across the expanse. It was a large reservoir with wide cleared areas surrounding it. Obviously trees had been cut—stumps were scattered as far as she could see.

Abrienda took a deep breath. She relished being back on the ground. Somehow she'd have to convince Vincente to renegotiate the bet. She didn't want to go up again.

Though all things considered, it hadn't been as bad as her imagination. No one had fallen out. The basket hadn't given way.

And she had been held closely for a brief moment by one of Barcelona's most exciting bachelors. Not that she had bragging rights. But for those few moments she'd felt totally safe.

She refused to think about the moments he'd held her hand and tried to charm her into joining forces with him. Best left in the past. It wouldn't be repeated.

Sighing softly for what could never be, she looked around, spotting a road winding down through the trees. When the chase crew arrived it would be from that direction.

She walked back to the basket.

"Now I'd like some thing to drink, please," she said.

Domingo tossed a soda to her.

"Something to eat, too?" he asked.

"In a little while. I'm hoping this will settle the butterflies in my stomach."

"You did fine, Abrienda. No need to be afraid," he said gently, leaning against the side of the basket, taking a long drink from the can he held.

"Phobias aren't something that go away on your say-so," she said.

She drank from the cold can, then looked around.

"No, I guess not." He was silent for a moment then turned toward her. "So why the Children's Home, to make the check out to?"

"You'll really do that?" she asked.

"I said so, didn't I?"

There was a hint of steel in his tone.

She flashed back to the meeting in her boss's office. Domingo had become angry with the slightest hint from Vincente that he wasn't honorable. Obviously that meant a lot to him, which struck her as odd, given the ruthless nature of every successful businessman. Was Domingo a bit different? Unlikely.

Abrienda had never had such a generous gesture made for her.

"My parents were both orphans. My mother actually lived in the Home for a few months when she was about eleven. It was a favored charity for them."

"And were your parents happy?" he asked.

"Yes. We did lots of things together as a family. It wasn't perfect. My mother had a real temper and she would let it fly rather than bottle things up inside. But ten minutes later the storm was over and they were hugging and kissing."

She smiled a bit at the memories.

"I want a relationship like that if I ever get married," she said, looking at the water, remembering the sudden storm that had swamped the boat they'd been on, ending their happy family life forever.

She shivered.

"I shall be happy to make the donation in their name," Domingo said, watching her.

The minutes dragged by. By feeding the hot air into the balloon periodically, enough to keep it from fully deflating and drifting to the ground, Domingo watched the gas gauge.

It was getting lower each time he fired the burners. If the propane gas ran out, the balloon would gradually sink to the ground. If that happened before the rest of the team arrived, he'd have to hope he and Abrienda could control the deflating envelope enough to keep it from catching in the trees.

Abrienda drank her soda and ate one of the sandwiches Maria had prepared.

"How far to the nearest town?" she asked, looking around.

"I saw one toward the east before we came down. I don't know, maybe ten miles."

Ten miles. Was there any traffic where she could hitch a ride? Now she wished she'd spent some of her time up in the air studying the layout on the ground.

Just as she heard the burners fire up again, she heard the honking horn and turned to see the chase team racing down the narrow road, horn blaring.

"They're here," Abrienda said, jumping up from the stump she'd been sitting. "We're rescued."

Domingo laughed.

"We didn't need rescue. We'll refuel and lift off again. This time you won't be so afraid. You know how it all works."

By the time the balloon lifted again, Abrienda hoped she would discover a way to be far gone.

But she didn't. Working in perfect synchronization, the team swapped full propane tanks for the empties, keeping the envelope almost full. In less than thirty minutes one of the chase team called to Domingo that he saw the other balloon.

"Oops, time to go," Domingo said. "Come on, Abrienda."

She wanted to argue, but the camaraderie of the ground crew and the pride she felt that she'd actually survived mellowed her thinking. If all these people thought the event worth taking part in, maybe she needed to give it one more chance.

And, truly, if she didn't look down, she had grown used to the gentle movement of the gondola and almost gotten used to the sudden noise when the burners were engaged.

She hadn't gotten used to Domingo, however. Still, she

could do this, what choice did she have?

She looked up and saw the other hot air balloon almost overhead.

"They'll get ahead of us," she said as she grabbed the jacket she'd discarded and hurried to the gondola. By the time they rose enough to catch the current, Alvarez's balloon had a slight lead.

Domingo turned his head to smile at her.

"We'll catch them if they get ahead. Fire up the fans," he called as he opened the burners and the roaring filled their ears. In only seconds the balloon began to rise rapidly.

Abrienda watched, her attention torn between their own efforts and the balloon sailing silently overhead.

"They're getting ahead," she said.

If her boss outdistanced Domingo the first day, would that settle the race? Glancing at the charged energy Domingo showed, she doubted it. He'd fight to the last second to gain even an inch of distance.

"You come and take the controls," Domingo said. "I need to consult the weather maps of the area. Keep the burners going until the temperature gets near the limit."

Abrienda stepped closer to the center. She grabbed the lever and pulled down, feeling almost like a pro. They were gaining altitude rapidly now. Soon they were level with Vincente's balloon, though some distance behind.

Domingo glanced up from the charts and maps he was perusing and looked around. He jotted a note on the margin of the paper.

The trees had dropped away, the surrounding hills were left behind. The burners roared and Abrienda laughed in sheer delight.

She'd done it. She wasn't about to go near the edge of the basket, but she'd lifted the balloon from the ground. Looking at the other balloon, she saw they were rapidly passing it in elevation. Would a different air current sweep them past?

She glanced at Domingo and found him grinning at her.

"Told you it'd get better," he said.

The euphoria she experienced allowed her to incline her head regally and agree.

"So you did. How long do we have to keep the burners on?"

"You judge. Keep an eye on the gauge."

Abrienda watched, and when it got close to the high temperature mark, she closed the controls. The silence echoed in her ears, ringing from the sound of the burners.

She kept her hand on the lever for balance and looked triumphantly at Domingo.

"We're higher than Vincente's balloon."

"Well done. Come here and I'll show you the route I think the currents will take us."

She hesitated a moment, glancing straight out over the side of the basket. But they were so high, she could see little. Her heart lurched and she quickly sat down beside Domingo. He held out the edge of the paper and she drew it closer.

Leaning near, Domingo pointed out the topography and explained how air currents rose and fell, some on different currents, some impacted by the terrain and the heat of the day.

His shoulder brushed hers and Abrienda caught her breath, forcing herself to concentrate on his words and following where his finger pointed.

Turning her head slightly, she saw the faint lines radiating from the outer edges of his eyes, as if he squinted in the sunlight a lot. His skin was tanned and taut, covering high cheekbones. His dark eyes sparkled with the excitement of planning where he'd try to take their balloon.

He glanced at her, and Abrienda quickly turned back to the map, trying to quell her rapid heart rate. Surely he could hear her blood pounding through her veins? Better if he thought she was suffering from fright than the true nature of her feelings. She was too much attracted to the man.

"Any questions?" he asked.

"How did you get involved in this?" she asked, daring to look at him again.

"This race or hot air ballooning?" he asked, standing and doing a 360-degree scan.

"I know how you got into this race, I meant the entire sport."

"It was something new to try and I liked it once I did."

"Flying airplanes and scuba diving isn't enough?" she asked.

He raised one eyebrow in silent question.

She refused to admit she'd been interested enough in him to look him up and find out about him before the race.

"I like challenging myself," he said at last. "And exploring unusual things. I'm thinking of taking part in an archaeological dig in the Holy Land next spring."

"At least that would be safer than depending on hot air to keep you above ground," she said. "Doesn't your family worry about your recklessness?"

He laughed. "No one worries about me," he said. "And

I'm not sure they'd consider what I do reckless, anyway. I'm not, you know."

"Now, how would I know that? I scarcely know you."

"I've been doing business for Alvarez since before you were hired."

"Maybe, maybe not. I've worked for the firm for more than seven years. It's only the last three I've been Vincente's PA."

"And before that?"

"I worked for another company. It didn't offer the chances for advancement that I needed. I do have my brother to care for, remember."

He nodded, his expression becoming thoughtful.

"What?" she asked as he kept quiet.

"I was wondering if my brother would have put his life on hold to watch out for me if we'd been in your situation."

"Why wouldn't he?" she asked. "It's what families do."

"Not all families. Some families don't stick together."

"I know your parents are divorced," she said. "Your father's mentioned enough in the papers."

Domingo laughed. "And you don't approve."

He knew that for a fact from her tone of voice. Her expression supported it, as well.

"His life has no bearing on mine. But don't you think it's not in good form for him to be dating women younger than you are?"

"As long as we don't get our wires crossed and date the same woman, then, no, I don't care."

"I would. Parents are supposed to be a good example to their children."

"I'm hardly a child," he said.

"You were at some point."

Not liking the trend of the conversation, Domingo rose and looked over the side of the basket. They were gradually losing altitude. Alvarez's balloon was farther to the west, and it was difficult to gauge if he was ahead or behind, since Domingo had lost track of where they were by talking to Abrienda.

"Bring the map and let's figure out where we are," he said, opening the burners and heating the air above them.

Abrienda slowly got to her feet and stepped closer, holding it out for him.

"Can you check the terrain and see what you think?" he asked.

"No."

She thrust the map at him and reached for the controls.

"You figure that out, I'll keep us afloat."

She didn't trust the amusement in his eyes, but didn't try to figure out what she'd done. Reaching for the knob, her hand brushed his and she felt the touch as if it had been a caress.

Oh, oh, bad, bad, bad. She drew a deep breath and looked everywhere but at Domingo.

She wasn't going to get some stupid crush on the playboy. That would be the dumbest thing she could do. Her immediate goal was to get back to earth in one piece and have a good night's sleep. Maybe tomorrow something would happen to end the race and let her return home.

Domingo calculated where they were and called the chase team. When he'd notified them, he handed her the walkie-talkie.

"Press this button to talk, release to listen," he said.

"What do I have to say?"

"Anything you want, I merely want you to know how to use it."

"Why?"

"In case something happens to me, of course."

Abrienda felt a flare of panic. "What could happen?"

"Nothing, this is just in case."

She stared at him as she pressed the button.

"This is Abrienda. Will we stop near a town that has a good restaurant for dinner?"

It was inane, but the only thing she came up with.

"We can hope, Abrienda," Marie responded. "And we hope for a decent hotel with hot shower and comfortable beds. Over."

Domingo took it back.

"We have air mattresses. No time to be locating five-star hotels. We have a long-distance race to win. Out."

He heard their laughter before the radio went silent.

"We're sleeping on the ground?" she asked.

"Not if I can help it. But it keeps them on their toes."

She nodded. He had a good relationship with his ground crew. Did he operate his business that way?

It was far different from the way Vincente ran things. He was the boss and he wanted everyone to know that.

The other balloon remained in sight all afternoon. Abrienda felt more courageous and, as long as she didn't look directly over the side, she was able to keep her fear of heights under control.

She enjoyed the distant views, watched the other balloon when it would move up or down, trying to see if Vincente or Domingo's PA was at the controls. Most likely Vincente. He didn't like to share the spotlight and would want bragging rights if he won.

At one point Domingo peered over the edge and called the chase team. It was time to switch out the tanks again and there were several wide-open spaces he thought would work.

This time the team was waiting when the balloon settled to the earth. Once again Abrienda was amazed at the precision exchange. They were airborne again within thirty minutes.

Late in the afternoon, Domingo called the ground crew.

"I see what I think is San Paolo up ahead. If so, there's a large soccer field on the outskirts. I'll see if we can touch down there."

There was momentary discussion among the ground crew, then Manuel came on and confirmed Domingo's estimation. The small resort town was in a valley between two mountain ranges. Abrienda had heard about it, but never thought to visit. It looked as if Maria might get her five-star hotel after all. Surely they wouldn't camp out if a hotel was that close?

She looked at the other balloon.

"Do you think they'll keep going?" she asked. Already Domingo was descending.

"I have no idea, but this is the best landing area around. I for one wouldn't take the chance on finding something else farther on before dark."

Even as he said that, she could tell the other balloon was beginning to descend.

"I'll be able to call my brother, right?" she asked.

"Yes. Are you worried about him? I assure you my housekeeper will take care of all his meals. Beyond that, he's well able to look after himself."

"I'm not worried, but I do want to check in with him. He's only seventeen. Besides, he'll have a million questions about today. I wish he'd been able to go in my place."

"Suggest that to your boss. Do you mother Jose a lot? In another year he'll be going off to university. Are you planning to accompany him?"

"Don't be absurd. Of course not."

Intellectually she knew she had to let her brother go. He was almost a man, had his own way in life to make. But it had been just the two of them for so long. Was this how parents felt when their children left the home?

"Didn't your parents worry about you and your brother when you left home?" she asked.

"I doubt it. We were sent to a boarding school from the age of eight. Neither seemed particularly concerned."

"I gather you aren't close."

He looked at her and slowly shook his head.

"Not close at all. I've only met my mother's current husband once. I avoid my father's woman of the week. He changes them too frequently to keep track."

"That's sad," she murmured.

"It's reality. Not that you have such a great life in comparison. No parents, no other family apart from your brother, and you're obviously struggling with money issues."

"I make a good living and support us just fine. There's money for Jose's university fees and he can also work."

She was insulted he thought her unable to provide.

"I only meant it must have been hard when your parents died and everything fell on you."

She hated to talk about that time. It still could cause nightmares. She'd been so scared of the future, so worried she'd not be able to take proper care of her younger brother.

"I managed," was all she said.

Chapter Seven

San Paolo was designed as a full-service resort catering to the wealthy from all over Europe. It was a short trip by car from Barcelona. It had taken the entire day by lighter-than-air balloon. There were spas, swimming pools, golf courses, equestrian centers, a soccer field and a plethora of fine restaurants.

The chase team was on-site waiting for the balloon when Domingo gently set it down. Moving with well-rehearsed efficiency, the team tethered the basket, and began aiding in the collapsing of the balloon. They folded it lengthwise several times then rolled it toward the basket. Throwing a tarp over it to keep off the evening dew, they were done in record time.

"Who got the short straw?" Domingo asked as he watched the activity.

"Julio," Maria said. She was already disconnecting the onboard propane tanks, handing the empty ones to Paolo, who stored them in the back of the truck to be refilled.

"Which means?" Abrienda asked.

"He'll stay with the balloon tonight to keep gawkers away. We can expect a crowd in the morning to watch us lift off."

"So he has to sleep on the ground, but we get the hotel?"

Domingo laughed.

"Indeed we do. Unless you want to stay out here to keep him company?"

She shook her head, to the laughter of the others.

* * *

Thirty minutes later Abrienda closed the door to the suite Domingo had assigned her. It was beautiful beyond belief. The sitting room was decorated in lovely shades of rose and lavender. The sofa was huge and comfortable she realized when she sat on it. Bouncing once, she jumped up and headed for the bedroom. It was complete luxury. A white-on-white monochromatic theme had gauzy curtains flanking the floor-to-ceiling windows. A mock canopy over the head of the bed with matching gauzy material floating to the floor gave it a fairy-tale feeling. The duvet was white with a brocade motif. There had to be a dozen large decorative pillows. It was spectacular.

She went to the bathroom and stared in amazement. It was larger than her living room. There was a spa tub and a separate shower with six shower heads at various levels. The glittering glass tiles sparkled in the light. Thick, fluffy towels filled a shelf and were also stacked in rolls on the wide counter. A thick terry robe was artfully draped over the wide bench in the center of the room.

Abrienda kicked off her shoes and was unbuttoning her shirt when her phone rang. There was even a receiver in the bathroom. She lifted it slowly.

"This is Abrienda," she said.

"I told you we wouldn't sleep on the ground." Domingo's voice came through loud and clear.

"So you did."

She clutched the opened shirt together.

"Is your room okay?"

"It's lovely, thank you."

She was glad he was footing the bill. It would have set her back two weeks' pay to stay one night in this place.

"We're getting together for dinner in an hour. We'll discuss tomorrow's ride and get an early night. Join us. Main lounge, one hour."

"Okay," she said.

Before she could say anything else, he rang off.

An hour gave her plenty of time to shower and see what she had to wear to dinner. Nothing suitable, she was sure. She'd crammed in clothes every which way when she'd had less than five minutes to dress and pack that morning.

Entering the lobby a short time later, Abrienda saw the rest of the crew assembled near the entry to one of the restaurants. She walked over, relieved to see everyone was dressed casually in clothes more suitable to outdoor activities than a luxury resort restaurant.

At least she wasn't odd man out.

"There will be a table for us in just a few moments," Maria said, when Abrienda joined the group.

While they waited, Vincente Alvarez and his crew came from the elevators. Abrienda hadn't known her boss was staying there, as well.

"Did we beat their distance?" she asked.

"Hard to say. Still, it's close enough to make it exciting.

They came down not far from us. This is the nearest place to stay," Manuel said.

Paolo excused himself and went to talk to Vincente.

In a moment Helena left that group and walked to her boss.

"How are things going?" Domingo asked his PA after she greeted everyone.

"Fine. I think I'd enjoy it more in your balloon. Vincente insists on doing everything, and he's obsessed with winning," Helena said.

Domingo shrugged. "So am I. He won't, you know."

"He thinks Abrienda will hold you up." Helena looked at Abrienda. "But it doesn't seem like you're trailing."

Abrienda frowned. "Why would I hold Domingo up?"

Helena glanced at Domingo then said in a soft voice, "Vincente's counting on your fear of heights to delay you. In fact, he said he was surprised you hadn't already bailed."

Abrienda felt a flare of anger at her boss. Was that the reason Vincente had proposed her. Not for her lack of experience but her fear of heights? Did he expect her to refuse to fly and force a win by Domingo's forfeiture?

A warm hand gently took her arm. Startled, she looked at Domingo.

"No need to tear his head off. The best revenge is to win and show him he misjudged you."

"I've worked for him for years and I'm annoyed he'd use me like that," she admitted.

"He wants to win."

"Are you afraid of heights?" she asked Helena.

She wasn't sure she cared either way, the warmth of

Domingo's hand seemed to infuse her entire body. Her temper cooled and once again she felt the odd tickle of awareness.

"I jumped at the chance to go when Domingo asked me," she replied. "It's turning out all right. As long as I just enjoy the scenery, I'm fine. Maybe before we reach the end I'll get to do more. Your boss strikes me as a bit of a control freak."

"I didn't jump at the chance," Abrienda murmured.

"But you haven't let me down. I won't forget that, Abrienda," Domingo said softly. It sounded almost like a promise.

Helena turned back to Domingo and said, "I checked for messages when I got to my room, which, by the way, I'm sharing with one of the chase team members. Gina said Teresa called for you and then asked for me. She seemed miffed neither of us was there to talk to her. She wants you to call her when you get the opportunity."

"Duly noted."

Helena grinned. "So, no return call tonight, then."

Abrienda listened, wondering if Teresa now regretted her decision to refuse to go on the week-long trip with Domingo.

She also absorbed the fact that Vincente was having his crew members share quarters while she had a luxury suite all to herself. Should she be sharing with Maria? She knew if that was the way Domingo wanted it, he would have made it that way.

She was grateful for her room.

Abrienda felt a bit bereft when Domingo released her arm after the maître d' announced their table was ready. Following them into the dining room, she sat between Manuel and Maria.

Paolo rejoined their group and before long meals were ordered. Conversation at the table centered on the race.

Looking around the restaurant, she wished Jose could see it. They'd never eaten in a place so elegant. Many of those present were dressed up, although of course neither their group or Vincente's were.

What would it be like to come alone with Domingo, dressed to the nines, fascinating him with her scintillating conversation? Just the two of them, maybe in that small alcove that seemed more private than the main dining area.

The dream popped when the waiter poured bubbly beverages and Domingo rose to offer a toast.

"To winning the race and besting the competition — always!"

"Yea!"

They all raised their glasses and then drank. Abrienda was surprised to realize it was sparkling apple cider. She blinked and took another sip.

Maria leaned closer and smiled at Abrienda's expression.

"We do not drink during the race. Nothing must hamper our abilities, you know."

She laughed and took a long drink from her own glass.

Abrienda enjoyed the lively discussion, analyzing the day's flight, making plans for tomorrow's leg. All the tanks would be refilled. New weather maps would be downloaded from the Internet and topographical maps reviewed. There seem to be constant work she never knew about when thinking about hot air ballooning.

"I checked the weather before coming down," Domingo said at one point. "We might have a problem in a day or two as there's a storm predicted."

"Will that hamper our flight?" she asked with concern.

"It could," Domingo answered. "The air becomes too turbulent to safely navigate. With downdrafts that could collapse a balloon, contradicting wind directions throwing the basket every which way, it's not safe to be airborne in a storm."

"Not to mention if you get zapped by lightning," Manuel murmured.

"Or getting rained on," Maria added.

"So we put down if it appears a storm is imminent," Domingo concluded. "Don't worry, I promised to get you home in one piece."

All the more reason for her not to be on this trip. Her visions of falling out and ending up as a splotch on the earth rose again. What if the storm came too fast, collapsed the balloon and they fell like a rock? She grew nervous thinking about it.

"Have you called your brother yet?" Domingo asked as the meal was ending.

"I plan to do so when I get back to my room."

After this sumptuous meal, she'd have even more to tell him. She'd make the event sound adventuresome. Jose probably wouldn't remember her fear of heights. He'd be too caught up on the facts of the trip and on how far they'd come. She'd have to tell him about firing the burners and could stretch reality a bit by telling him she was fine on the journey.

The group broke up once they finished eating. Most of them headed for the elevator, one or two going for a quick walk or to peruse the gift shops.

When they crossed the lobby, Abrienda glanced around and stopped when she saw her boss holding court with several reporters.

Domingo stopped with her, following her line of sight.

"Couldn't stand not to be in the limelight," he murmured.

"You think he arranged this? We didn't know where we would be stopping for the night," she said, watching as her boss appeared in his element, fielding questions, giving a larger-than-life account of the day's events.

"It was pretty easy to predict by mid afternoon how far we'd get. And there aren't a lot of places around here to stay. I think he'd have traveled a lot farther than we did to have his moment in the limelight. I can't wait to see him at the end of the last day. He won't be so anxious to give press interviews. Did you want to join him?" Domingo asked.

"Good grief no."

He flung an arm casually across her shoulders and turned back to the elevators. While they waited, he leaned close and said, "Be sure to get enough rest tonight. We'll head out before dawn. Leave a wake-up call with the front desk so I don't have to come get you."

Like he had that morning.

Abrienda nodded, feeling conflicted. She liked his arm across her shoulders. She didn't like his autocratic orders. She almost felt as if she should salute him. He must have caught a glimmer of annoyance in her eyes, because he leaned closer and said, for her ears only, "Think of it as besting your boss. You'd like that, wouldn't you?"

"It's a toss-up. By besting him, I'm aiding you."

He was so close she was getting dizzy.

"And I'm the enemy?"

His eyes sparkled with amusement.

Abrienda felt herself grow deliciously warm. Her heart rate increased. This man was dangerous to be around. They were cocooned in a world of their own. His body blocked the rest of the lobby. She could only feel her heart race and the weight of his arm. He'd moved slightly so she felt sheltered in his embrace.

"Perhaps not precisely an enemy, but certainly not a friend."

She licked her lips and watched as his eyes followed the movement. He licked his lips in reflex and she could imagine feeling them pressed against her own.

"Maybe that will come. We have six more days," he said, his gaze holding hers.

Become involved with one of the wealthiest businessmen in Barcelona? Totally unlikely, especially if he truly wanted more than friendship. But she smiled at the odd notion. Wouldn't that be something to tell her friends, casually mentioning Domingo Ortego in conversation? She almost laughed aloud imagining her friends' reactions.

The bell announcing the elevator shattered her foolish thoughts.

It was dark when the wake-up call came. Abrienda struggled with the desire to go back to sleep, but knew Domingo wasn't past demanding security open the door and admit him so he himself could drag her from bed, so she reluctantly got up and dressed as quickly as she could. Tossing everything back into her bag, she was ready five minutes ahead of time. Leaving the room, she rode an empty elevator to the lobby.

The lobby was quiet and subdued compared to last night. Even the lights were dimmed. She took her bag to the large entrance where a bellman took it and soon had it stored on the chase truck. Most of the crew was already standing by the truck talking and they greeted her cheerfully. When Domingo joined them a few seconds later, they took off for the field.

Abrienda was better prepared for today's outing, though she constantly scanned the sky to see if there was any sign of the storms they talked about. The stars shone brightly everywhere. Not a cloud in the dark expanse.

Her anxiety rose as the balloon filled. She gratefully took the mug of coffee someone handed her, sipping the hot beverage and hoping she could cope again today. She was a bit proud of herself for sticking with it yesterday. Even though fleeing to a town would have been impossible, she was glad she hadn't tried.

Even Jose had been encouraging during last night's phone call, after asking her for every detail. Telling her how lucky she was to be able to make the long jump.

"Ready?" Domingo asked.

She glanced at him, taking in the fact he looked wide-awake and excited. Obviously waiting in the dark didn't dampen his spirits at all.

"As I'll ever be," she said, holding out the empty cup to one of the crew as they walked by.

"I hope by the end of the trip you don't look as if you're going to the guillotine every time you approach the basket."

"Maybe if you had some phobia, you'd be more sympathetic," she replied smartly.

"Maybe my phobia is losing, something I don't intend to

explore. Let's go. We can get an early start on Alvarez today. They were still at the hotel when we left. If we ride the wind just right we can gain more ground."

"It's still dark," she said, once in the basket and watching as the team released the tether lines and slowly began to grow smaller beneath them.

The jets roared. The glow in the balloon was the only light around until they rose high enough to see the streetlights and windows of the resort.

"It'll be light soon enough. Watch the eastern horizon, you'll see it's lightening there already. No power lines around, nothing but clear skies and smooth sailing and, we hope, a fast wind," he called over the sound of the burners.

Standing near the side, still an arm's length away, Abrienda didn't feel the fear she expected. Instead she felt a sense of anticipation. It was odd to look out and see dark rolling hills silhouetted against a starry sky with few scattered lights on the ground below. There was no sense of height or distance in the diffused light of early dawn. She should enjoy what she could. She'd never do something like this again.

Turning, she stepped next to Domingo.

"Tell me what I can do."

"About?" he asked.

"Winning this race."

That surprised him, she could tell.

"Interesting. Why the change of heart?"

"What, that I would want to win? I'm competitive, too."

"What happened to your calling it a stupid race?"

"Nothing, it still amazes me that two grown men would wager an extraordinary amount of money on a hot air balloon race, but after Vincente's comments last night, I'm definitely switching loyalties for the duration. Besides, you have a fan in my brother. He suggested I reconsider my stance and give my team my all."

Domingo said nothing, just studied the other balloon in the distance as it began to rise.

"There's nothing to do now, but you can spell me later on the burners."

Could he trust her? Domingo wasn't one to give his trust easily. He'd learned as a child to guard that which was his and count on no one but himself. Still, how much damage could she do unless she deliberately sabotaged something? Which was unlikely, as afraid of falling as she was.

"Fine."

She crossed to the corner, stacked the two blankets and sat down. As long as she was below the level of the basket she wasn't as scared, but he wished she could enjoy the ride.

The sun was peeking over the horizon, bathing the earth in pure light. It was one of the joys he found in the sport. Gliding silently above the world when the burners were off.

Abrienda leaned back against the basket, confident today it wouldn't give way and let her fall. In fact, when she thought about things this morning, she realized she hadn't felt the body-numbing fear she had yesterday.

The notion brightened her outlook. She felt almost in charity with Domingo, forgiving him for forcing her on this adventure. As Jose had said, there were lots of people who paid for balloon rides. She was getting one for free.

Once the balloon reached the height to satisfy Domingo, he shut off the burners.

"Want something to eat?"

"I thought we were skipping breakfast."

"We picked up some croissants before we left."

She happily unwrapped the food while Domingo poured hot coffee from a thermos. In only moments they were enjoying a high-altitude picnic. She watched as he stood and kept looking around.

"So what made you challenge Vincente to this bet?" she asked.

"For the chance to win."

"What if you can't?"

He laughed. "Of course I can. Today we out-distance him, and by day five he won't even see us we'll be so far ahead."

"How can you be so sure?"

He studied her for a moment, then shrugged.

"Vincente's a show-off. He does spectacular stunts for notice. He's never done a long jump before. And we're away from crowds and media, last night notwithstanding. Those were local reporters, no one from Barcelona was there. Granted the news story went out over the wires, but we're not going to find a luxury hotel to stop in every night. Once there's no one around to show off for, he'll grow bored, and I'm hoping, sloppy in his efforts."

"While you're as driven as if this really meant something. Which it must, but I can't figure out what. You don't want the money, you've already said you'd donate that. So what do you get out of winning?"

"The satisfaction of beating him, and ramming home the point in front of the entire Barcelona Business Alliance."

"Is this some kind of revenge?"

He hesitated a moment, then said, "Just a way to put a man in his place."

Abrienda thought about that for a while. She knew the company had had dealings with Domingo's company since before she began to work for Vincente. But she'd seen no sign of bad feelings between the two men, as long as she discounted the tension surrounding their meetings.

Was it pure competitiveness? Each wanting to be the alpha male? She experienced a bit of that with her brother and his friends. Always jockeying for leader position of their group, they were friends yet rivals.

Yet something more than that drove Domingo, she was sure of it. What was it?

"I can almost see the wheels spinning in your mind," he said.

Taking a last swallow of coffee, he put the cup in the bag and fired the burners for a few seconds to maintain their altitude.

"I can't figure you out," she said with some vexation.

"And you need to because why?"

"I like things tidy."

She scrambled to her feet, pitching her own empty cup into the small bag and then cautiously looking around. The other balloon was some distance away. Other than that one, the sky was empty. It was another lovely cloudless day. She wondered if there would be bad weather later.

"Let's just say it balances things out," Domingo said at last.

Sounded cryptic to her. She watched the horizon for a while, then went to sit back in her corner.

Abrienda was getting used to the slight rocking motion and the alternating noisy and then quiet times. She was also getting a bit bored, sitting where she could look up and see the balloon, or looking around and seeing the four sides of the wicker basket and the man who'd brought her along.

"Tell me more about your family," she said after a long stretch of silence.

"What's to tell? I have a mother, a father and a brother. He's married and has two children."

"The end? That's all? I've read about your father, but I don't know much about your mother."

"There's no reason you should."

Feeling rebuffed, Abrienda lapsed into silence. She'd go bonkers if something didn't liven up the day. Maybe she could call Maria on the radio and have a decent conversation.

But not a private one, she knew. And she didn't quite see Domingo meekly allowing her to monopolize the airways.

In fact, she couldn't envision Domingo ever being meek.

"I had my parents until I was in university. Their death was unexpected, but we had a strong family bond until that moment," she said. Maybe if she started the conversation, he'd open up.

"Lucky you."

He stooped down beside her. Abrienda glanced at him.

"Shouldn't you be watching—where we're going or how close to the ground we're getting?"

"We're going where the wind takes us. We're high enough not to worry about obstacles, and when you think we need to rise some more, you can handle the burners."

She scooted a bit to the left, not wanting to be so close to him. It was uncomfortable that her body seemed to think Domingo was the greatest thing since sliced bread while she knew intellectually that he was far beyond her league. She was no comparison to the lovely Teresa Valquez for instance. And she wasn't sure she ever wanted to be. The idea of being escorted around for a few weeks or months and then left behind when he moved to another woman was too uncomfortable to imagine.

Abrienda waited a moment, then stood, keeping as close to the center of the basket as she could. They were quite high. Still, a check of the gauge showed the interior balloon air had cooled and she daringly reached up to turn on the burners for a half-dozen seconds.

Domingo watched her but said nothing.

She felt quite competent.

They talked through the morning. Abrienda couldn't help jumping up more frequently than Domingo did to check their height from the earth. And scan around for anything that could impede their trip.

The other balloon seemed lower and was veering in a different direction. One time she ventured to look straight down. Her heart caught in her throat and she felt an impending urge to keep moving over the edge of the basket and fall to earth. She dropped to the floor and tried to catch her breath.

"You okay?"

"I looked down," she said, her eyes tightly closed.

She wasn't going to fall out of this balloon.

Patiently she waited for the waves of nausea to pass. She wouldn't look down again she'd be okay if she didn't look straight down.

Domingo grasped her shoulder with one hand.

"Abrienda, you're perfectly safe here. I would never let you come to harm.

His hand rubbed her gently. She opened her eyes. He was right smack in front of her. Close enough to give comfort and a feeling of security.

Close enough to kiss.

The thought popped into her mind and she almost groaned with the temptation. His dark eyes watched her carefully, trying to calm her nervousness.

The fear of falling faded and another emotion took charge. One of tempting the attraction she felt to push the boundaries and see if Domingo had any interest in her. It wouldn't be the same as in Barcelona. No press was hounding them. They were alone for hours at a time. She could let down her guard a little and see what happened.

Which would be totally stupid. Sanity regained the upper hand.

"I thought you were doing better," he said.

"I was, then I looked straight down."

"So don't do that."

She nodded. "You'd think I'd remember that."

"Come on, have a drink and take the burner, take your mind off your phobia."

"Heights don't bother you?"

"No."

"Is it true you scaled Mont Blanc a few summers ago?" she asked, reluctantly standing back in the center, hoping she could concentrate on other things besides the huge amount of empty space between her and the earth.

"I did."

She'd read that recently in one of the reports on the Internet.

"Wasn't that a bit scary?"

"I called it exhilarating."

"Dangerous, rather. You could have fallen and been killed."

"Danger gave it an extra fillip of excitement. I never thought about dying on the mountain."

"But it *could* happen."

"Of course it could. But I could also be killed by a truck running a red light in Barcelona," he replied, leaning casually against the side of the basket.

"I guess. But to deliberately put yourself in danger, that's just weird."

He laughed. Her heart skipped a beat.

"I like some excitement in life. No crime in that."

"Reckless," she commented.

He shrugged, his eyes dancing in amusement.

"Maybe. But it's my life to do with as I will."

"Since you have no family to worry about."

"Families are overrated."

The amusement vanished in an instant.

She blinked.

"If I hadn't had my brother when my parents died, I don't know what I'd have done. We don't have any other family, just long-term family friends. Which in a way we consider an extended family. You're lucky, you still have both your parents and your brother."

He took another swallow from his can, then studied it a moment before looking at Abrienda.

"You were stuck raising a boy when your parents died. Where's the luck in that? You're still young. You should be out having fun. Doing a job you love instead of working for Alvarez."

"How do you know I don't like that job?"

"You said you'd change it if you could."

"I love my brother. I told you, if not for him, I'd be alone in the world. Though I do hope to marry someday."

"Ah, the great panacea for life."

"What do you mean by that?" she asked curiously.

He crushed the empty soda can and put it into the small trash bag. Looking around, he made sure things were going according to plan and then looked back at Abrienda. She looked around, trying to see what he did. Should they go up some more? She opened the throttle and the jets roared. The balloon rose.

He watched her, making her feel funny. When she felt the balloon move, she realized they'd risen into another current. The basket actually swayed a moment and she fought to keep her balance. Fear flashed. She took a deep breath, reassured by Domingo's casual pose.

Once they stabilized, she grinned. She'd held her ground. Quite an accomplishment for her.

"Don't you believe in marriage?" she asked then.

"It seems to be all right for some, but not all. Look at my parents. They married in the heat of passion when young. Once the passion faded, they didn't even like each other much. Too bad they didn't think of that before having two children."

"Yet you wouldn't be here if they had," she murmured.

"Would the world be worse off because of that?" he asked.

She was shocked. It was not something she had ever considered. Whether the world was better off because she lived.

"Maybe not, but you have the opportunity to do good."

"Oh, oh, Miss Crusader. Like what?"

"If nothing else, you'll donate a lot of money to a children's charity. And I know your company gives to various organizations in Barcelona," she ended triumphantly.

"So how does my father benefit mankind?"

She laughed.

"I'm not saying everyone has to. Maybe his sole purpose was to produce you."

Domingo laughed at that.

"Right. And my mother's sole purpose? Besides seeing how many men she can marry before she's too old to appeal to anyone."

"Oh, you're so cynical. Maybe she's searching for happiness and doesn't recognize it when she's got it."

"Pop Psychology 101," he retorted. "Maybe she's a wealthy, bored woman looking for thrills. I like mine on the mountain side."

"Or in a hot air balloon," she answered.

He inclined his head in agreement. "It's a different kind of sport but satisfying all the same."

Domingo watched as Abrienda assimilated his comments. He could tell she still had starry ideas about marriage, love and happy ever after. He wished her good luck with that. In his experience it was truly rare.

Maybe that was the problem. His experiences were limited. If Abrienda were anything to go by, he'd missed an entire category of women. She was unlike anyone he'd dated in the last ten years. Maybe ever.

Of course their circumstances were unlike any other. He knew she didn't want to be with him. Was it the novelty of that idea that intrigued him? He'd become accustomed to the attention of beautiful women. Was he jaded? It'd be unreasonable to expect all women to fall over themselves for a chance to be with him.

But it irked him that Abrienda didn't. He could offer her so much more than anything she'd had so far in life yet she remained aloof and distant. He didn't understand her.

"I feel sorry for you, Domingo," she said slowly.

Her eyes showed the sympathy.

He felt a flash of surprise. "Why?"

"Because you're missing out on the best part of life. Finding someone to share your joys and sorrows and to go through life together. My parents loved each other very much and my mother once said she could put up with anything as long as she had my dad in her corner. Who do you have in *your* corner?"

Chapter Eight

"Any one of a number of friends," Domingo said calmly. But was it true?

He had many business acquaintances, some casual friends to go to parties with or sail with. But except for Phillip Stanton and Marco Valdez from school days, he had a superficial relationship with most people. It'd even been a number of months since he'd spoken to Phillip or Marco.

Or his brother.

For a moment he wondered what special tie connected Abrienda and her brother. Banding together in the face of tragedy? Would he put his life on hold if Andreas needed him? Domingo liked to think so, but he began to wonder if Andreas would reciprocate.

"Good for you," she said, looking out at the other balloon. "How long before we stop again?"

"Another two hours, I hope. The air is cooler today, meaning it's easier for us to get lift with the hot air. As long as the propane lasts, we're good to go."

She sighed.

"Hey, this is a perfect chance to see Spain from the air. You're missing a lot by not taking advantage."

"Like heart attack, nausea, fainting."

He laughed and crossed to her side. Taking her hand in his, he pulled her closer to the side.

"I'll hold on to you to keep you safe," he said as he positioned her near the wicker, but not too close.

Wrapping his arms around her, he pulled her back against his chest, leaning over slightly to rest his chin on her shoulder.

"Look at that. It's hard to imagine all that open land when we live in such a crowded city."

Abrienda slowly let her eyes drink in the view. It was breathtaking.

Domingo was right, it was lovely. Slowly she turned her head to see as much as she could. When she turned it the other way, she bumped into Domingo's face. His cheek was warm. She could feel him smile.

"Nice, huh?"

What, the view?

Or being held by him, feeling safe and secure and almost cherished? She savored the moment. His arms held her securely to his rock-solid body. His feet were braced to balance them in the slight sway of the basket. She could let go of her fear and enjoy the spectacular vision spread out beneath them.

And her senses were far more attuned to the man holding her than to her fear of falling. It was a delight to savor the moment. She closed her eyes and tried to imprint every detail on her mind to remember through the rest of her life. Soaring over Spain, held by Domingo. Her real life faded into the background. For these few moments, this was all that was real.

By the time Domingo found a spot where he could safely put down the balloon, Abrienda was more than ready to stop.

A person could only stand being on edge for so long. She wanted to run on the ground, get away from his disturbing presence and touch base with reality.

Her boss's balloon had put down twenty minutes earlier. She was beginning to suspect he didn't carry as much fuel as they did. So they, once again, gained some distance, but Vincente could easily catch up and pass them while they exchanged tanks. They were still too close to predict any clear-cut winner.

The chase crew was already in the clearing, which Abrienda found amazing.

Once the balloon was down and secured, a festive picnic lunch was served and quickly eaten as everyone stood. Using a GPS indicator, Domingo calculated the distance they'd already gone.

"Do you think we can make another one hundred miles this afternoon?" Julio asked.

"If the wind holds. It kicked up once or twice."

"A problem?" Manuel asked.

"No."

Abrienda finished her meal.

"I'm going for a quick walk. Being in that confined space gets to me," she said.

Maria offered to go with her.

"Thanks, but unless you really want to, I'm fine. I'll look at the scenery from ground level and relish not being airborne for a while."

She flicked a glance at Domingo.

"We leave in ten," he said.

She started off along the road the truck was parked on. It

was hard packed dirt and easy to walk on. It'd grown warm and she left her jacket at the picnic area. There was plenty to do to ready the balloon for the next leg, but the others were far more competent than her.

And she needed some time to herself. Being with Domingo felt like a roller-coaster ride. She disliked being in the balloon yet she was captivated by her pilot. She resented his autocratic ways yet she yearned for a kiss.

That stopped her. She shook her head and started walking again. The very last thing in the world she needed was to be kissed by Domingo. She had a feeling it would spoil her for any man in the future.

And for him it would merely be another woman in a long line of women. He'd probably forget her name by Christmas.

Sighing softly, she tried to count her blessings and hope something would happen to speed up the race.

Abrienda was about to turn around when she heard a vehicle behind her. Stepping to the side of the road, she stopped. It was the chase truck. Domingo was driving. He stopped even with her and looked at her through the passenger side window.

"You walking home?" he asked easily.

She shook her head and opened the door. Climbing in, she looked at him.

"I was just walking. Has it been ten minutes?"

She wasn't wearing a watch, but surely she hadn't been gone that long.

"Nine. We'll be back in a sec and take off again."

"Did you really think I'd try to walk away?" she asked. She hated being his partner, but she wouldn't let him down, because she was starting to also believe her boss needed taking down a peg or two.

"No. But if you twisted your ankle or something, it'd have been hard for you to get back. Feeling better for the walk?"

"Yes," she said.

It took only a moment to return to the balloon. Maria had a phone to her ear. When she saw the truck, she said something to Paolo and then headed to meet Domingo.

Abrienda hopped out of the truck and watched as Maria came up to Domingo.

"The office is trying to reach you," she said, holding out the phone.

Domingo took it. "Make it quick," he said. A moment later he bit out an epithet. "Under no circumstances tell her you've talked to me. If she calls again, tell her you'll relay the message and that's all. Put Jaime on the phone."

Domingo walked away talking to the man on the other end.

Maria grinned at Abrienda and said, "Girlfriend troubles."

"Teresa Valquez?"

"Yes, she keeps calling. I think Sophie is getting fed up with all the messages she's left. Guess now Miss High and Mighty wishes she hadn't thrown away her chance for the long jump after all. Though she was not a ballooner. You never heard such complaining."

Abrienda vowed to keep her own thoughts about ballooning to herself. She may not like it, but she didn't want to give rise to gossip.

Domingo was impatient to begin the ride. Abrienda scanned the sky. There was no sign of the other balloon.

Maybe they'd maintain their lead.

Once in the basket and beginning to lift, she asked Domingo, "Do you think Vincente will have reporters there again tonight?"

"I wouldn't put it past him," Domingo said, eyeing the balloon.

Abrienda wasn't able to judge their rate of ascent since she kept her eyes inside the basket and had nothing to gauge it by. She enjoyed watching Domingo when he was concentrating on something else.

When he turned off the burners, she looked around. Still no sign of Vincente's balloon.

"So we got a jump on him this leg," she murmured.

"Enough to keep the lead, I hope."

Abrienda stood in one corner and leaned against the propane tank.

Domingo took the map from one of the storage pockets and began to study it.

"Shouldn't you be watching?" she asked.

"I'll check it soon. You let me know if we're going to crash into anything."

She looked at the empty sky. They were far too high to worry about power lines, even if there had been any around. The other balloon was lifting in the distance.

"The scenery aside, there's not much to do, is there? Are the festivals like this, too?"

Domingo shook his head and began telling her about the ones he'd attended. She liked listening to him as he talked, closing her eyes to concentrate better.

"Am I putting you to sleep?" he asked.

"No, I listen better with my eyes closed," she said.

The last thing she felt around him was tired. She could feel the heat from his body. She could smell the unique scent that would forever be imprinted in her mind as Domingo's.

Wishing she could record his voice to listen to years down the road, she smiled as he told her of the antics and contests at the festival. His description was romantic and dramatic, and surprisingly the stories did not all feature him as the star.

He fired up the jets and she opened her eyes to watch him.

He was tall and slender, with broad shoulders and a tapering waist. His hair had been permanently disheveled since they started. She liked it. It made him seem that much more approachable.

By the time he switched to the last propane tank, dusk was drawing near. Domingo constantly scanned the horizon, but there was no place in sight to set down. The last thing he wanted was to have to land in the dark. There was no telling what dangers there'd be.

Maria called him on the radio, the signal poor and staticky.

"Lost sight of you…different direction…we can find."

"Say again," he replied.

"You are going in a different direction from the road. We can't find a way to cut over. Do you see a landing site?"

"Negative."

He glanced behind him but didn't see Alvarez's balloon. The man had been behind all afternoon and had probably put down at the wide area Domingo had seen about a half hour ago. He looked ahead again. Still nothing suitable.

Static again. Then"…us your GPS coordinates. We'll find…"

Domingo glanced at the GPS device and then relayed the coordinates, saying them slowly and then repeating them.

"Got it."

Domingo clicked off the radio and glanced at Abrienda. He expected to be reproached or have her complain or say again she was frightened.

But she watched him calmly. Was that trust he saw in her eyes?

"So I'll do the burners if you watch for a place to land," she said, stepping close to him.

He let her hand brush against his when she reached for the lever. He was playing with fire to entertain any thoughts of getting involved with Abrienda. She was content in her life and had her brother to raise. Heck, she probably didn't even have a dress suitable for some of the places he liked to take women.

Though that wouldn't be a problem. He could buy her whatever she needed. He knew enough from the talk at social events who the leading designers were, where their gowns could be purchased.

Then again maybe he'd take her for a weekend sail, just the two of them on the sea. No need for fancy dresses there.

Frowning at the way his thoughts were going, he took advantage of her offer and rummaged in a side pocket for the binoculars he carried. Finding them, he began to scan the direction they were going. There had to be something opening up soon.

Had he been with one of his chase team who had experience in the balloon, he wouldn't be as concerned. Meeting all challenges was one of the things he liked best about the sport. One couldn't plan out as with plane flights. Meeting the unexpected and handling it was exhilarating. Or it would be, if he wasn't constantly aware of his passenger and her fear of heights. The last thing he wanted was to give her any reason to fear during the flight.

There, in the distance, he saw an opening in the trees. He lowered the binoculars and tried to gauge how far it was and when they should start down. They had far outdistanced Alvarez today. Tomorrow he'd get even farther.

In less than twenty minutes they were on the ground. Abrienda jumped over the side and grabbed a tether rope. There wasn't the need to find an anchor quickly this time, as the balloon was deflating, with nothing nearby to cause a problem.

Once the tug from the breeze died, he jumped over the side with her and took another rope, securing the basket.

"So we just stand here?" she asked.

"For a few minutes. The envelope is already almost down."

"It's not going to cover us, is it?"

"It won't hurt if it does, we can crawl out. But, no, it'll go the other direction. There, it's almost down."

When the nylon was lying on the ground, Domingo dropped his rope and indicated Abrienda could do the same.

She did so, hesitantly.

"Good job," he said, joining her.

"Now what?"

"We wait for the others."

She looked around. "I don't see a road."

"They'll come."

"We are not where we were when you gave them the GPS location."

"Manuel and Maria both know how to calculate distance and direction. And we have a beacon that I can start that gives off a signal. When they're close enough, they'll receive that. I haven't been wrong yet, have I?"

"Not that I know of, but that doesn't mean you can't be," she said, annoyed with him.

He looked as fresh and energetic as he had that morning.

She'd love to sit somewhere and relish being on the earth again. She knew any hint of makeup she'd put on that morning was gone. Her hair had to be a mess. And she'd love to forget about everything and just veg out, preferably away from Domingo Ortego.

He laughed. "True enough. But better for my image if every time I'm wrong, few people know about it."

He looked around, fists on his hips.

Abrienda thought he looked the way a conquistador probably looked when landing in the New World and thinking he'd conquered all he surveyed.

"We can wait in the basket if you like," he said.

"No, thanks, I've spent enough time there today."

"Then help me with the balloon."

They stretched it out, folded it and then began rolling it toward the basket. Once it was compacted, he reached in the basket for the blankets and a large plastic tarp.

"We cover the balloon, then we sit and wait."

"Why cover the balloon?"

"To keep it dry. Wet nylon doesn't inflate very well."

"Oh."

"I'll take a blanket to sit on," he said when the envelope was covered. He also pulled out the last two sodas.

She handed him a blanket and then put hers down on the ground. Domingo sat opposite her.

"Will we have to spend the night here?" she asked as he tossed her one of the sodas and kept the other.

"Probably. I didn't see any signs of civilization when looking for this space. I don't want to spend a lot of time traveling back and forth when we could be airborne."

"I'm not much for camping," she said.

"Ever been?" he asked.

She shook her head.

"Then how do you know?"

"I like hot and cold running water too much."

"Look on this as a great adventure."

"Yeah, that's what my brother says. Who says I want adventure?"

Domingo laughed.

Abrienda swallowed her drink wrong and ended up in a coughing fit. He pounded her on the back until she stopped.

"Thanks, I'm okay now."

She looked around. The clearing was several acres in size. There were a few scruffy trees here and there, but otherwise it was a rocky flat area on the dry side of the hills they'd been following all day. She was already feeling the hard unevenness of the ground beneath her. How could she sleep on it? How could she sleep alone with Domingo?

Were there wild animals? She looked around, realizing how fast the light was fading.

"It'll be dark soon," she said.

"We have a couple of flashlights in the gondola. At least when it's dark, you can see the stars like never before. Each one is crystal clear."

"I'd think you'd dislike it even more than I do. Aren't you missing the fancy restaurants like last night? The luxurious hotel with the fabulous spa tub?"

"You've been reading too many newspaper accounts. Sure I enjoy fine things. And I like eating good food. But I also enjoy climbing, hot air ballooning. Versatility's needed for both."

"So tell me about climbing. How did you get into that?"

"Friends from school and I first went on a trek in France when I was around eighteen. I was hooked. Talk about a challenge—finding my way up the face of a cliff that looked as if it had never been scaled. Reaching the summit and feeling like I was on the rim of the world. You should try it sometime."

Abrienda shook her head in horror. "I can't imagine anything much worse. Unless it's hot air ballooning."

"So your hobbies are needlepoint or knitting, safe and secure?"

"Don't turn your nose up at those kinds of hobbies. They're probably fun for many people. But not for me. I like computers."

"So you don't take your brother on camping trips?"

"Is that a guy thing? He does plenty outside. He's going on a science camp this week, with twenty other students. They'll be camping out and exploring geophysical phenomena. He'll love it, even if it rains."

"I do admit to preferring four walls and a roof in the rain,"

Domingo said.

He stretched out his single blanket, then lay down.

"Are you going to sleep?" Abrienda asked.

It was getting darker by the moment. She could already see a few stars in the sky.

"No, just wanting a good view of the sky. Once the crew gets here we'll have a fire and lights and miss some of the spectacle."

Domingo confused her. Every time she thought she understood him, he'd say or do something opposite to what she'd expect. There was more to him than the playboy image he seemed to relish in Barcelona.

There was something rock solid about him. Even when he pushed for his own way, she knew she could count on him to keep his word and get her home safe.

She looked at the sky. If she sat looking up long enough, she'd get a terrible crick in her neck. Reluctantly she spread her own blanket and lay down. Shifting slightly to find a more comfortable spot she relaxed and enjoyed the starry sky. The darker it became, the more stars appeared. She could see the Milky Way.

"It's spectacular," she murmured.

"It always puts things into perspective," he said.

"Like?"

"Like work is not the be all and end all of life. That we are insignificant creatures in the great scheme of things. How many stars can you count?"

"I can't count them all!" She laughed.

"They say God knows the name of every star."

"I find that totally amazing."

She was silent for a moment savoring the beauty above her.

"You could have asked for the fifty thousand Euros for yourself," he said.

"What?" She sat up. "Where did that come from?"

"I was thinking about your scathing comments about the bet. I'm sure you must have imagined what that kind of money could do for you and your brother."

"I provide just fine for me and my brother. Soon he'll be on his own and every penny I earn will be mine."

"A gift, then," he said.

"No, thank you. That's not my style."

He looked at her, silhouetted against the night sky.

"So what is your style?"

"To earn my own way," she said.

He smiled, though she couldn't see in the dark. So idealistic. Refreshing after the women he usually dated. Then again, maybe the fault lay in his taste in women.

"After this balloon ride, maybe you'll feel you earned it. Or at least a bonus from Alvarez for going above and beyond the duties of a PA."

"Are you giving Helena a bonus?" she asked.

"Yes."

No need to tell her the thought had just come to him. Helena made a good salary, but this was certainly above and beyond.

"Money plays a big part of your life," she said slowly.

Her voice moved as she lay back down.

"It does in everyone's life," he replied.

"Not so much in ours, mainly because we don't have a lot.

And we need to save for when Jose is at university. Besides, it mainly buys things. Not memories."

"Like?"

"Like the afternoons at the beach we used to enjoy with our parents. We'd spend all day playing in the water, picnicking, being together. I miss those times. And holidays, when we celebrated together."

"You paint an idyllic life. Real life doesn't follow that."

"Your parents didn't do right by you and your brother."

"So you're now an expert on my parents?" he asked. The old wound threatened to reopen. He knew she was right, but years of hiding the disappointment he'd felt at being shunted to school and holiday resorts while his parents went their separate ways resurfaced.

He'd never subject a child to that. Which was why he planned to stay single all his life.

"Money can buy memories," he argued, just for the heck of it. "Making enough to afford my interests is satisfying."

"So you try flying, either by plane or balloon, and scuba diving, racing. High-adrenaline sports," she said. "Sounds like something's missing."

"Nothing's missing. I do well in business and can indulge myself with any sport I want."

"If you were married, you'd have a family to build memories with. What happens when you're eighty and can't do all those sports?"

Domingo laughed. "I doubt I'll want to if I live to be eighty. And I will have the memories you put such store in."

"But who would you have to share them with?"

"Who do you have?" he countered.

"Jose for one. And I do hope to marry someday and have a family. Children to love and raise. A husband to grow old with, to share my life and his."

"I can't see my parents sitting on a veranda somewhere in thirty years swapping stories about the good old days."

"I bet my parents would have. With grandchildren around. That's sad your parents don't have family memories."

He sat up, not wanting to continue this topic.

"Not sad, just fact. What about people who don't have a happy life, do you think they want to remember that when they get old?"

She fell silent.

Domingo stood and looked around. It was dark with no ambient light but that from the stars overhead. He could make out the silhouette of the rim of hills behind them. No roads, but plenty of open land for Manuel to drive over. He hoped the GPS locator was functioning.

"Hungry?" he asked.

"A little."

She sat up, drawing the blanket over her shoulders. It was growing cooler.

"We have some snacks left. But dinner will have to wait on the crew."

"And that could be six hours away," she murmured.

"No, they'll be here before long."

"If not?"

"Then we bunk down here."

"Just the two of us," she said softly.

"Do you have a problem with that?"

"Should I?"

"Depends on what you consider a problem."

Abrienda's heart rate sped up. She imagined a lot of scenarios. None of which she'd classify as precisely a problem. Unless she considered being stranded with one of Barcelona's more infamous bachelors a problem.

"Look on it as a great adventure."

"I don't think I'm the adventurous type."

"Then it's time you break out of your mold and see what you find," he said. He sat beside her and nudged her slightly with his shoulder. "Live on the wild side for a while. Explore new things, push yourself. Find out who you really are."

"And who are you, Domingo?" she asked.

"Someone hoping to go through life experiencing many different facets. Like sailing, soaring, kissing beautiful women."

The low, sexy tone had her senses on full alert. What would it be like to be kissed by an adventurer?

She was about to find out, she thought, feeling giddy and breathless at the idea.

"Abrienda?" he said softly, brushing back her hair from her face, turning toward her.

She saw his head blot the stars then felt his lips brush across hers.

Decision time. Should she scoot away and be outraged, or give in to rampant curiosity and indulge herself as he suggested?

He gathered her closer, blanket and all, and moved past the mere brush of lips for a full-fledged kiss that had her blood pounding through her veins, her head spinning and her own hands reaching out to grasp his jacket and hold on.

The hard ground was forgotten. He shifted slightly, bringing her even closer in his embrace as his tongue teased her lips, dancing with her own when she opened to him. Abrienda felt like a top spinning. It was glorious. No wonder women vied to date the man. He set a new standard in kissing.

Too soon he pulled back a bit, his breath fanning her cheeks.

"Sorry, I couldn't resist."

Sorry. She pushed against that rock-solid chest and scooted back, suddenly feeling every pebble and rock beneath her. Disentangling herself from the blanket, she stood and moved even farther away.

"Try exercising more control next time you feel you can't resist," she snapped.

She turned, tears of humiliation threatening.

"Hey, Abrienda, it was only a kiss," he said, coming up behind her and putting his hands on her shoulders. "I didn't mean anything," he said.

That was the problem. It was the best kiss she'd ever had, and he didn't mean anything.

He stepped up and leaned his head next to hers. She felt the warmth from his cheek next to hers.

"I'm sorry if you're upset. I won't do it again."

Probably not. He was used to gorgeous sophisticated women, not some overworked PA who had to be forced to go on this race with him.

"I think we should keep this businesslike," she said stiffly.

She really wanted him to turn her into his arms again and say nothing was more important to him than her. She almost laughed at the expression he'd have if she voiced that crazy idea.

"I agree. Friends?"

"I doubt we can ever be friends. Just let it drop," she said, shrugging out of his hold and stepping away.

She dare not go too far, as she had no idea where anything was in the darkness.

Would they end up wrapped in the blankets, sleeping beneath the stars? At least the storms he mentioned hadn't materialized. That would really be horrid.

The silence grew awkward and she knew she hadn't handled things well. But she couldn't risk getting too comfortable with him or she'd make an idiot of herself over the man, and then where would she be? She had her brother to get off to university and her own dreams to pursue.

It was almost thirty minutes later that the first glimpse of the headlights shone through the trees.

"Is that them?" she asked, jumping up and trying to see more than flashes of lights at ground level.

"Probably." Domingo went to the basket and retrieved the radio. In seconds he was in contact with the crew and turned on both flashlights to show them where they were. In less than twenty minutes the truck arrived, lurching over the rough terrain, illuminating everything with its powerful headlights.

Abrienda was so glad they'd arrived. She needed a buffer between her and Domingo.

Camping had never been high on her list of things to do, but with accomplished veterans, it turned out to be fun.

The meal was cooked and shared by all. The crew and Domingo checked out the balloon, exchanged the propane tanks and made everything ready for the morning flight.

Then air mattresses were inflated, sleeping bags doled out and in less time than she'd expected, Abrienda was warm and sleepy. She watched the sky for a few minutes, then closed her eyes and went to sleep. To dream about Domingo's amazing kisses.

Domingo lay in his bag, watching the sky, thinking of the earlier kiss. He'd done it as a lark; only, it'd backfired.

Abrienda hadn't seemed to enjoy it, while he'd enjoyed it far too much. Who would have thought Alvarez's PA could kiss like that? He wanted another taste, another kiss to see if what he'd felt had been a rebound from Teresa or if there was a special spark there.

Unlikely, he thought sardonically. Abrienda just didn't approve of his lifestyle. And to top it off, she wanted marriage and children and memories.

He was making his own memories. Doing things most men only dreamed about.

He thought about the various things he'd tried over the past few years. Turned out this balloon race was the best of the lot, and it was all because of his reluctant passenger.

Domingo frowned. Abrienda was no more special than any of the other women he'd seen over the past decade. She was pretty in a very unpretentious way. Perhaps lacking the sophistication he was used to made her a novelty. Yet she was genuine. Like the woman his brother had married.

But that'd change given half a chance. Abrienda could be seduced by diamonds and couture clothing, embassy parties and luxurious cruises. He knew what women liked. It was all well and good to talk about family and memories.

He'd like to see her dressed in a beautiful gown, jewels

glowing around her neck, hair elaborately done. He could take her to a reception, or maybe a Christmas ball. Show her a different side of Barcelona than she knew.

And then what? Move on again? It was what he did.

They were airborne at first light. Abrienda had been avoiding him while they prepared for liftoff. Yet she was friendly with the crew, joking and laughing. It was only with him she became distant. And Domingo knew the others had noticed.

The balloon filled and tugged at the land-tethered gondola.

"Turn us loose," he said.

In seconds the ropes had been released and they began to soar. He kept the burners going full blast to heat the air to the maximum in the shortest time possible, and the balloon rose swiftly.

She sat in the corner, gazing up at the balloon. Without standing, there wasn't a lot to see.

The other balloon wasn't in sight. Satisfied he'd made a leap ahead of Alvarez, he wanted to keep that lead. The farther ahead he got, the better he'd like it.

By mid morning Domingo was tired of the silence. Abrienda had dozed for a short time, and when she wakened, he beckoned her over.

She rose and glanced around. He could tell she was easier each day with their height. He felt a moment of regret that he'd forced someone so afraid to come up, but he'd honored the conditions of the bet.

"Take over. I'm getting a drink," he said.

She nodded and stepped in his place.

"Want something?"

"Sure," she said.

Then she opened the throttle and the jets roared. The balloon rose even higher.

Domingo smiled. She was getting used to it in a big way. Looking at a spot on the horizon, he estimated their air speed. They were being pushed by a current at a faster rate than he expected. Since the balloon gave little indication of movement, it was hard to gauge the exact air speed.

He searched for the other balloon. Taking the binoculars, he trained them behind them until he located the other balloon. It was quite a distance away.

"We're going to win this easier than I thought," he murmured.

"Great, my boss will be a bear in the office if he loses."

"Prepare yourself."

He raised the binoculars again and frowned.

"What?" Abrienda asked.

He lowered them and looked at her.

"Storm clouds on the horizon. That bad weather front they talked about might be coming."

Abrienda held out her hand in silent request for the binoculars. When she lifted them to her eyes and trained them on the distant horizon, she saw the clouds. They didn't look particularly threatening and were right at the edge of the horizon. How long before they'd catch up? Wouldn't the air current they were on keep them moving ahead of the storm?

She asked Domingo.

"They will to some extent, but it depends on if the storm front is moving faster than this current."

Domingo contacted the ground crew. They had refilled the propane tanks and were heading in his direction. Domingo gave their GPS coordinates and told them to contact him when they were below him, which Manuel said should be soon.

"Now what?" she asked.

"Now we see where to land to exchange tanks. And if we can outrun the storm," he said.

Chapter Nine

Abrienda relinquished the controls and went to stand on the side of the gondola facing the clouds. Staying an arm's distance away, she watched as the sky gradually grew more and more cloudy, some fluffy white puffs, others long and dark. She could scarcely see Alvarez's balloon, and shortly before lunch, she lost sight of it altogether.

"Are we stopping soon?" she asked.

"No. The temperature is cooling, we can stay up longer. We have propane, we'll go as far as we can."

She caught a glimpse of a town. Holding on to the side, she looked at it.

"There's a town down there."

"We'll push on a bit farther."

"Good grief, don't put down in the mountains. The chase team would never find us."

"Sure they will. But that's not my intent. If we can get another few dozen miles, there is an entire valley that'd be perfect to set down in. And there's a nice-size town at the head of the valley. We could have a hot bath and comfortable bed tonight."

"That gets my vote," she said.

Turning, Abrienda watched Domingo as he stood

opposite her, leaning casually against the side. She no longer feared he'd fall out. In fact, thinking back over the last day or two, she realized she wasn't nearly as fearful as when they started, unless she looked directly down.

"Now what's going on in your mind?" he asked.

"Just thinking that maybe, *maybe* mind you, this isn't the worst that could happen to me."

He laughed. "It's exhilarating."

"I still can't look down, but I've stopped panicking every time the basket sways a little."

"We can make a ballooner out of you yet."

"I doubt that. Tomorrow will be the halfway day. After that, it's all downhill."

"Do you regret coming?" he asked.

"Not as much as I thought I would," she replied.

He nodded. "I knew I could count on you to be honest about it."

She looked away. She hadn't been honest about her feelings for that kiss. If he wanted the truth, she'd be hard pressed to comply. Some things were too personal to share.

"Abrienda, would you go out with me when we return to Barcelona?"

She turned back at that, stunned he'd ask.

"Where?" was the only thought that sprang to mind.

"Ballet, reception, dinner for two, dancing. Wherever you want."

For one breathless moment she wanted to say yes. Then she shook her head.

"I'm so not your type."

"And what is my type?"

He had to ask? Lounging comfortably against the side, he personified gorgeous male. His body was trim and muscular, his skin tanned from so much time in the sun. His hair was thick and dark. Her fingers actually itched to brush through it, feel the texture, savor the right to do just that.

"From what I saw of Teresa Valquez, about the opposite of me."

"Ah, a new dress, some strappy high heels and a diamond or two and you'd rival Teresa. Actually, your conversation far surpasses hers. She's more concerned with being seen in all the right places."

"You don't believe she cares for you?" she asked, startled at his comment.

She knew she didn't measure up, but she didn't need him suggesting she get new clothes and jewelry. Which she wouldn't do, even if she had the money.

"She cares for me because of my money. If I were a cabana boy, she wouldn't even give me the time of day."

She blinked, wondering if Domingo had ever worked on the beaches around Barcelona. She'd love to see him in a swimsuit, all glorious tanned skin and sleek muscles.

"There is an even larger gap between me and you. What makes you think I wouldn't date you for your money?"

"So far you seem singularly unimpressed by it. When faced with fifty thousand Euros, you wanted it to go to charity and you asked for nothing for yourself. Think how that money could help Jose in university."

"We can manage on our own," she said.

She wasn't some gold digger. If that was the type of woman he was used to, she felt even more sorry for him. But she wasn't joining the ranks of women he dated and discarded.

"So I'll buy you a pretty dress or two, a few baubles, and we'll go out," he said.

"No. Thank you for the invitation, but I buy my own clothes and I won't go out with you."

He tilted his head slightly. "Why not?" he asked softly.

She shook her head, not wanting to have to say anything more.

"Just no? There has to be a reason," he pressed.

"Just no."

He crossed the short distance and stood beside her, lifting her face to his with a finger beneath her chin.

"Why?"

His gaze seemed to bore right into her mind. Fortunately, he couldn't see the jumble of emotions swirling around in there exacerbated by his touch. She licked her lips and his eyes caught the movement.

"You're too dangerous," she said at last.

"Because?"

"Come off it, Domingo, you're just bored. You don't really want to date me. You've already made me over into a Teresa clone in your mind. If you wanted to take me someplace, you'd take me as I am, not try to make me into someone else."

He studied her for a few moments, then nodded and released her.

Abrienda took in a deep breath. She clenched her fists and tried to casually turn away, lest she forget all reason and jump into his arms.

The balloon spun around, fast enough to catch their

attention. The gondola swayed a bit with the sudden motion.

"What's wrong?" she asked, grabbing on to the side.

He leaned back to look at the envelope. Then, looking around, Domingo went to the burners and turned them on full blast.

Abrienda turned and saw the clouds were closer, a lot closer. She cautiously made her way to where he was standing.

"I think we've hit the leading edge of the storm front," he said calmly.

The sky was growing dark gray behind them. Obviously the wind, which one couldn't see, had outpaced the clouds. It was more turbulent than any they'd experienced before.

It wouldn't take long for the sun to get behind the clouds. She looked for the other balloon, but couldn't find it.

"Do you think Vincente already put down?"

"Highly likely. Whatever else, he isn't a fool. Take the controls and keep the jets going until you reach the high temperature."

He picked up the radio to contact the ground crew. Manuel responded, but once again there was static on the connection. Domingo asked for an update to the weather, in which direction the wind would be blowing and how long before the storm mass would become critical.

The response wasn't reassuring. The front was moving faster than originally anticipated. The leading winds should keep the balloon away from the rain and lightning for a while. His advice was for them to put down as soon as Domingo found a safe haven.

"How far away are you?" Domingo asked.

"We are tracking you by GPS now, but we haven't seen

you in a while. I'd say you've picked up some speed with the storm front."

Dom looked over the side, studying the ground. Hilly, no open meadows, and rocky in some places. He could set down if he needed, but the lack of roads and rough terrain made it highly unlikely his chase team would find them anytime soon. It'd taken them hours last night. He'd rather set down near civilization.

"We're heading north-northwest. Anything on the map in that direction where we can put down near a town?"

"Checking."

Abrienda watched him with wide eyes.

Domingo winked at her to keep her off balance. The last thing he needed was for a scared young woman to hamper the flight. She'd done well so far, despite her phobia about heights. He hoped she could hang on a bit longer.

If he were flying with Manuel or Maria, he'd be exhilarating in the speed, in racing the wind. The sky was clear ahead, there were no towns or airline flight paths or obstacles to hamper them. But if the storm came faster than the wind pushed them, he'd have to put down, rugged terrain or not. Trees or not. Abrienda's safety would come first. And second, the safety of his balloon.

He wasn't conceding yet.

"If you keep on your course, there are some plateaus in a few miles. But no paved roads lead to them and from your GPS position, you're about twenty miles west of us. There might be some sheep herders in the area. I don't know. We will keep on this direction. If you change directions, send the signal as arranged."

"Roger that. I'll let you know."

"What is an arranged signal?" Abrienda asked when Domingo put the radio down.

"Every half hour. Saves batteries, and they'll be monitoring at the exact times."

"And that works? Did we do that last night?"

"No, I've never had to use it. Don't plan to today, either."

Domingo could tell from the shadow racing across the landscape they were moving faster than before. Once or twice the balloon faltered, indicating traverse winds. He wasn't sure whether to rise or go lower to seek steady winds. One last look around convinced him he was ahead on this leg of the trip.

Carefully watching the balloon, Domingo kept busy trying to gauge the speed and pressure on the envelope. Abrienda was proving to be more help than he'd expected. She kept the balloon elevated. The wind spun them around again and she gave a short gasp, but didn't desert her duty station.

She did look at him with those wide eyes, questioning silently.

"We'll look for a place to set down," he said at last.

Watching in the direction they appeared to be going he searched for any open area. Snagging the balloon on tall trees on the way down could render it inoperable. Something he refused to do. There were several more days left on this flight and he planned to make the farthest distance when the week ended. He radioed his plans to the ground crew.

Abrienda jumped. "Oh, lightning," she said.

He looked behind him. The storm was still miles away, but another flash of lightning demonstrated the strength and danger coming.

"We'll start dropping now," he said into the radio. "Find us."

He tossed the radio down and turned to Abrienda.

"Don't fire the burners unless I tell you to."

Glancing behind him from time to time, he knew they were ahead of the rain. He wanted to be on the ground and erect some kind of shelter before the full force of the storm hit. They couldn't afford to get the envelope wet. It would take a day or more to dry out and that would definitely put them out of the running.

Abrienda didn't say a word. She watched his every move. He wished he could reassure her, but only being safely on the ground would do that.

The basket swayed more strongly than before. He heard Abrienda's gasp but was too intent on getting them down to do anything more than tell her to hold on and be ready to start the jets if he wanted more lift.

The balloon spun around, the basket swinging with the momentum. Even Domingo was having trouble holding his balance. The last sway had knocked Abrienda off her feet. She scrambled up and held on to the frame, looking over the edge, her face white.

The gusts were stronger the lower he went.

"Are we going to crash?" Abrienda asked.

"No."

And, surprisingly enough, they didn't. He reached a large plateau, pulled the emergency release cord and told Abrienda to be ready to jump off the basket when he gave the word.

"And take one of the ropes with you. I'll follow and pull on the other."

The basket hit hard, the balloon almost puddling over them as it continued its waffling in the wind as it collapsed with lack of hot air.

Abrienda jumped off and looked for something to tie the rope to. Domingo was beside her in a second, pulling on another rope.

It was windy.

Abrienda felt her cheeks stinging from the sand particles in the air as the wind swept across the rocky plateau.

The basket tugged against the rope. There didn't appear to be anything handy to anchor the rope.

Domingo strained to hold his rope even as Abrienda ran a few steps to keep the rope from being pulled from her hands. She got a better grip and leaned back, throwing her entire weight against the pull of the wind.

The envelope settled into an uneven lump, ruffled by the wind, but no longer driven by it. The pull on the rope eased. Abrienda was breathing hard, but held fast.

"Good going," Domingo called.

He studied the terrain, and then moved to the left a bit, trying his rope to an outcropping of rock. Not a very substantial one, from Abrienda's viewpoint, but she trusted Domingo knew what he was doing.

He crossed quickly to her side, taking the rope from her hands. He found another rock and made it fast.

"Let's do what we can before the rain comes," he said, already moving to the balloon.

Before long he had it stretched out, flapping in the wind, but in the wind's direction, with the basket as anchor. He began folding it, first length ways, then when it was as wide as the basket, began rolling it toward it.

As soon as Abrienda realized what he was doing she went to help, keeping a wary eye on the clouds massing behind them. Before they'd finished, the first drops of rain began to fall.

"We'll turn the basket on the side, floor to the storm's direction and huddle inside to keep dry," Domingo said, using one of the lines to fasten the balloon, scrambling for the plastic tarp and stretching it over the balloon. He stood and looked around. There was no shelter in sight.

"Help me tip the basket on its side, it'll afford some shelter."

Once that was done, he sent Abrienda to sit in it, while he double-checked the jets and then found a large rock and dug a shallow trench around the covered balloon.

In seconds he joined her in the makeshift shelter, the one side away from the wind open to the elements. The rest was cozy and so far dry.

"If the storm gets very bad, the wicker will leak," he said.

"But we stay with the balloon," she said.

"It's the best way for the crew to find us," he explained.

"How will they know where to look for us?"

"They'll find us."

They sat and waited.

"Is there a road to this plateau?" she asked.

"I saw a dirt one not too far away. Every half hour we'll use the radio and see if we can raise them. They'll get here, sooner or later."

She was quiet for a moment.

"I think you enjoyed our ride down," she mused.

He laughed, flinging an arm across her shoulders.

"It's exhilarating, man against nature. Especially when man wins this round. I didn't expect the storm to come so quickly or to be caught without adequate shelter, to be honest. But we'll manage."

"It wasn't so bad. It all happened so fast, I didn't have a chance to become afraid."

"You did well, Abrienda. I'm glad you were with me instead—"

He cut himself off, but Abrienda knew he was thinking of Teresa. For a moment she felt pleased she'd done better than the other woman would have. But only for a moment. Then the obstacles to getting safely to some hotel for the night made themselves felt. She had a feeling it'd be a long time before his chase team located them.

"I've never been a big fan of camping out, as you know," she said. "So I really did get my fill last night."

"We have snacks, blankets, shelter. What more do we need?"

"I can think of several things, not the least of which is to be dry. This shelter may start to leak before long."

"We'll manage."

Abrienda wished once again she wasn't on this expedition. But not one to bemoan things beyond her control, she gave in to the inevitable.

She studied her companion. "Do you camp often?" she asked.

He studied the rain as it began to come down.

"Not if I can help it. I like my amenities too much. But now and then. Today's not good weather. But when it's clear, to be away from the city lights, to see the stars and feel the awesome vastness of space, it's well worth minor inconveniences. Admit it, once you had dinner, last night wasn't a total waste."

He puzzled her. She'd expect him to rail against the weather, to vent frustration on the circumstances. Instead, he seemed to take the setback in stride. Maybe even relish it a bit.

He reached for the radio and made a call. No one responded. He tried again, but again there came only static. Switching it off, he tossed it back on the pile they'd made on one side of the tipped basket.

"Might as well make ourselves as comfortable as possible," he said.

He stacked the blankets side by side and sat down. Patting the one beside him, he waited for her to join him.

Eyeing the dubious shelter, she wondered how much longer before the wicker began to leak. Even as the thought came to mind, a drop landed on her nose.

"I think our shelter is getting soggy," she said.

Domingo looked up and swore. He turned and rummaged through two of the pockets on the side, coming up with another plastic tarp, not as large as the one covering the balloon, but large enough. He went into the rain and tied it to the side of the basket now their roof, fighting it and the wind until he had it covered.

Crawling in, he brushed off his jacket, wet at the shoulders, and sat down.

"Won't the wind blow it off?" she asked, hearing the plastic snap as the wind slapped it against the basket.

"Might get some nicks and tears, but nothing major. I

think it'll hold. I'm more worried that water will get on the balloon. We need it dry to fly."

The bright idea came that perhaps both balloons would be too wet to fly again and the men would call off the bet. Or decide on the result based on where they had landed today. Then she could get home.

"Cold?" he asked.

"Getting there," she said.

She could sit on the blanket or wrap it around her. She wished they'd brought one of the sleeping bags.

He pulled her closer, next to him, and threw his blanket over their legs.

"Combined body heat is better than both of us freezing. Later, you'll have to give up the comfort of sitting on that blanket for added warmth."

They sat in silence for a few more minutes.

"The interesting thing about you, Abrienda," he said at last, "is that you rarely complain. This isn't the way I envisioned the race. You'd have every reason to complain about the circumstances, the weather, everything."

"It's hardly your fault the rain came."

"That doesn't stop some people."

He reached out and took her left hand.

"You're cold."

He engulfed both of hers with his own, which were much warmer.

"For the most part I'm comfortable," she said. Or as comfortable as she could be snuggled up to Domingo.

"Let's spread the other blanket."

"Then we'll be sitting on the cold ground, with only the

wicker between us."

"Then, this is what we'll do."

He encircled her shoulders again and pulled her partway across his chest, looping his other arm around her waist.

"Better?" he asked.

He was like a warm furnace, generating enough heat to keep both of them warm all night long, she thought.

"Thanks."

The wind howled. The drumming of the rain on the plastic sounded unusually loud.

Slowly Abrienda began to relax. She was warm, dry and safe. Granted no one knew when the chase team would arrive, but they'd showed up last night and would surely arrive before long today.

"So tell me about this family you hope to have one day," Domingo said just as Abrienda was thinking about trying to sleep.

"And open myself up to sarcasm? You've made your position clear."

"Hey, just because marriage isn't for me doesn't mean it's not for other people. I do have a couple of friends who seem to be making their marriages work. So what's your timetable? Marry by thirty, have two point three kids and get a large flat with a roof garden or something?"

"I have no timetable. There's no guarantee I'll ever find a man to love. Or one who will love me. But if I do, I'd want a full family life. Wherever we could afford to live would be fine. Though I hope it's near the water, I love the beach."

"I could take you sailing one day," he murmured.

She ignored his comment.

"Then, when the time is right, we could have some children. I know I'd like a couple. I liked having a younger brother. But I'd have mine closer together than my folks did. There are almost eleven years between me and Jose."

"But lucky for him there was that much time. You were able to raise him, keep your family intact."

"You're right. That's important."

"So what will this dream husband be like?" Domingo asked curiously.

She frowned.

"Probably unlike anyone you know," she said. "Solid, down-to-earth, grounded. He'll have a good job, and like to spend time doing family things, both when it's just us and then after the children arrive."

"No fancy parties, exotic vacations?"

"A week or two traveling each year might be nice. There're a lot of places in Europe I'd like to visit."

"But no camping," he said, his mouth right by her ear.

She shook her head. Though she'd never forget sleeping beneath the stars last night. Or the kiss they'd shared before the others arrived.

"So what do you see as your future? Dating different women every month, getting older while they get younger? Don't you get tired of such a superficial life?" she asked.

"You're more cynical than I thought," he said.

Domingo didn't like the picture she painted. He had been going out less and less frequently in the last couple of years. He didn't mind spending time alone and it suited him to read a good book or watch something worthwhile on television rather than a constant round of parties or social events.

"Like father, like son," she murmured.

Was that how others saw him, as careless and clueless as his father? The man couldn't settle on one woman, he was always dating new and even younger women.

"Do you ever wonder what older men trying to cling to their youth find to talk about with younger women? There have no shared histories of events. Music is probably different," she mused.

"Some women will say whatever a man wants to hear, just to keep him entertained."

"Good grief, that would drive me nuts. I want honesty in both parts," she said.

"I agree."

One reason he dated for a while and then moved on was the inane conversations he often ended up with. Yes, Domingo, of course you're right, Domingo. He could hear the echoes of their sultry voices. What he wanted was someone to stand up to him. Challenge his glib statements. Argue with him sometimes.

He suspected Abrienda was exactly the kind of woman to challenge any statement she didn't agree with. He couldn't see her as a yes-woman even to her boss.

"How do you and Vincente get along?" he asked, testing his theory.

"Fine. He tries to get his own way in things, and succeeds for the most part, but not with my off hours. He's very controlling, but I draw the line sometimes."

It fit the image Domingo had of Vincente Alvarez. The man was a control freak and driven, to boot.

But not as much as Domingo was, which showed in their

respective bottom lines.

Their talk during the afternoon ranged from mutual likes in music to differences in books they'd read. While coming from different backgrounds, they discovered they had similar ideas in entertainment—except for Domingo's extreme-sports bent.

Later hunger drove them to raid the snacks. Abrienda felt the chill of the day when Domingo no longer held her close. They ate quickly and then naturally moved back together as if they'd been a couple for a long time.

The afternoon passed slowly. The rain settled into a steady beat on the plastic roof.

"Tell me about your home," she said at one point, wishing to learn as much about him as she could. When would she ever have such a chance?

"It's up on the Via della Rosa, overlooking the city and the sea. It's primarily built from stone with lots of glass. I bought it about eight years ago. I have a housekeeper who keeps it in order for me."

"It's large, I suspect," she murmured.

"Too big for one man, but it's also an investment for the future. I expect it will appreciate in value and then I'll sell it for a profit."

"Do you see everything in profit and loss instead of it being your home?"

"I'm not there that much."

Domingo had no special attachment to his house. It pleased him to live there, but if he sold it tomorrow, he'd find something else just as suitable.

"Besides, it's just stone, wood and glass."

"A home should be a special place. Comfortable to give you rest, secure to give you safety, a place to shut out the world."

"And your little apartment is that?" he asked.

It looked cramped to him.

"As close as Jose and I can make it. It was different when we lived at home with our parents. Our house there was so lovely."

She fell silent for a moment.

Domingo felt a stirring of envy. She and her family obviously operated entirely differently from him and his. He tried to imagine what she described and felt a hint of frustration. Not everyone was cut out to find a special bond as her mother and father had. Look at his own parents.

"Will you stay there once Jose moves out?" he asked.

"I might. The rent's affordable, though I'd love to have a place with a garden and perhaps a view of the sea."

He had acres of land, gardens galore and a sweeping view of the Mediterranean Sea. Would she like his house if she saw it? He frowned. He rarely invited women to his place, preferring to keep that part of his life his own.

Yet he wished he could see Abrienda's face when she saw the garden and the view. He bet she'd love it. And he'd love to show it to her.

Would the house appeal to a woman? Probably not as he had it decorated—with sleek modern furnishings. What he'd seen of her apartment was cozy, slightly cluttered and definitely not modern. Yet it had held a certain appeal even for the few moments he'd been there.

In fact, that was what made Abrienda different from the

other women he normally associated with. She was more old-fashioned than trendy, at least in family views and in decorating skills.

By the time it grew dark, Domingo had tried numerous times to reach Manuel, to no avail. Not having proper attire for the rain, the visits outside were brief and it took too long to warm up once back in the make-shift shelter.

They ate more of the snacks before it got too dark to see. He wanted to use the flashlights sparingly to save the batteries. He had faith in his crew, but not knowing where the balloon had set down, it'd be difficult to locate them in the stormy weather.

"We're going to spend the night here, aren't we?" she asked.

"I didn't see any towns nearby," he said.

The one thing about Abrienda, she was easy to be around. She didn't rail against fate for things going the way they were. She didn't complain or voice her frustration with the circumstances. He couldn't imagine spending the night under these circumstances with anyone else.

"If the rain ends by morning, and the envelope didn't get wet, we can inflate the balloon ourselves. We have enough propane to get airborne and stay there for a little while. We'll plan to stop at the next town or field near a road so the others can locate us," he said.

"I hope it's a town. I want to call home before Jose leaves on his school trip. If we don't make it early tomorrow, I'll miss him."

"He knows we don't always know where we'll set down for the night," Domingo said.

"He's the one who should have come on this trip, he'd love it." She sighed.

"But you're getting used to it," Domingo commented.

She'd changed, whether she knew it or not. He enjoyed holding her against him. Her slight frame fit perfectly against his. They had to sit sideways, with the wicker behind him, his feet touching one of the propane tanks. It wouldn't be the best way to sleep, if it came to that, but they could manage.

"I am getting used to it, and that's astonishing. I can't believe I'm not sick at the mere thought of going so high each day. As long as I don't look down, I'm really okay."

She looked over her shoulder at him. "But don't get ideas I want to do this again. If you hadn't forced me—"

"Hey, blame your boss. I was just making sure I got a fair shake at this bet."

"I plan to. We shall have words," she promised.

Domingo grinned. Anything to cause disruption with Vincente Alvarez worked for him.

"You're not like I thought you'd be," she said slowly, tilting her head back down and wiggling slightly to get comfortable.

"And how was that?"

"Arrogant, self-centered, uncaring, riding over anyone and anything in your way. Not that you don't act that way sometimes—like forcing me on this trip. But I've watched you with the ground crew. You aren't like that with them. You don't brag all the time or put on airs. Or boss people around. You treat them with respect. They know their jobs and you let them do it."

Domingo laughed aloud at that.

"They'd put me in my place in a heartbeat if I tried to tell them what to do. They're my friends, Abrienda. Not close, but we all share a mutual interest in ballooning. Manuel and Julio have taken the balloon up when I'm not around. I trust them implicitly."

Abrienda nodded as if a question had been answered.

"Put on airs?" he said, amusement dancing in his eyes.

"Vincente does all the time, like he's king of the world or something. He really likes the attention and adulation."

"Don't compare me to Alvarez. He and I are totally different."

"I know. But on the surface, initially, you two seem a lot alike. Except—"

He waited, wondering what she would say next. She was very open, letting her emotions show every time. Whether she was happy, sad or angry, there was no doubt. A person knew exactly what she was feeling just by looking at her.

"You have a stronger sense of ethics, I think," she said slowly. "I've noticed it more than once. If anyone challenges something you say, you get angry instantly. That old saying, a man's word is his bond—you take it seriously, don't you?"

"Of course."

She nodded. "Why? So many people today are more cavalier, not caring about others, or even what others think about them. Why is that so important to you?"

"To be different from my father," Domingo said.

The words were out before he could think.

She frowned in confusion. "How so?"

Now he had to explain. Better if he'd kept his mouth shut.

"As a child I heard endless times he would be taking me

and Andreas out someplace special. Then something would come up and he'd go off and leave us. Time and time again."

The old anger brushed him. He'd sworn as a young boy to never say anything he didn't mean or couldn't live up to. He knew what disappointment was.

"Your father's so different from mine. He loved spending time with his family. Why have kids if you aren't going to spend time with them?" she asked.

"I've often wondered that. Probably to leave the family fortune to."

"It could always be left to charity. Children deserve more than monetary inheritances, they need love and nurturing from their parents, grandparents, aunts and uncles. Everyone in their lives."

"Life isn't like that. It sounds like a fairy tale," he commented.

"It should be like that," she defended.

"So how long into your marriage do you think you'll make it before you change your mind?" Domingo wondered aloud.

"I wouldn't."

"People are basically selfish. My parents didn't like being tied down with the demands of children. They hired nannies to keep themselves free to do what they wanted. When we were old enough, we were shipped off to school."

She pulled away and turned to look at him.

"That is selfish and self-centered. Once you have children, they should come first in your life until they're grown. It's not as though your parents' lives ended when you and your brother were born. Childhood's fleeting. Once you reached a certain age, they'd have been totally free to do what they wanted. Would it have been too much trouble to put you two first for a few years?"

"For them, yes. Not for your parents, evidently."

She felt passionate about this issue. For a moment Domingo wanted to say he shared her views. He knew his parents had been too extreme in denying their children. Yet it was the only way he knew. He didn't know them very well and they certainly didn't know him, though his father was pleased with the success Domingo had achieved. But he thought only as a reflection on him.

"I think my parents loved us enough to enjoy being with us. Maybe because neither had family of their own, they wanted that bond. Mama miscarried twice between me and my brother, yet they kept trying to have more children. They really wanted us," she said.

"And you'll be that kind of mother, too? Having children to complete your life, putting them first?"

Dumb question, of course she would. She was doing it with her brother, so how much stronger the maternal bond would be with Abrienda's own children.

She narrowed her eyes.

"I plan to be the best parent I can be. As you will, as well, I expect."

That startled him.

"I don't plan to marry," he said abruptly.

"What if you fall passionately in love with someone and want to spend your life with her?"

"I'm thirty-four years old. I haven't met anyone yet, and I don't expect to."

"You never know."

"Oh, so now you're the Delphic oracle?" he teased.

She shook her head in exasperation.

"I'm trying to make a point here. If you do get married and have children, you'll probably be a terrific father."

"Whoa, where do you get your ideas?"

"From you."

"I never plan to marry, so how would I have children?"

She looked smug.

"Because you are one of the sexiest men on the planet, and women must fall over themselves to be with you. Sooner or later you'll find one you can't resist."

Domingo laughed.

"What a picture you paint of me. I do not have women falling over themselves, though the notion has merit."

"Maybe you're just blind to what's going on," she suggested.

"You confuse people who want what they can get from me with people who want to be friends with me. There's a decided difference, you know."

Abrienda was quiet for a moment. She hadn't thought about that.

"Is it horrible—never knowing if someone is with you because of your money?" she asked.

"Not horrible. But, if I don't trust anyone, how could I marry?"

"You'll know. When you do marry, you'd cling to that with all you have. And you'd be the kind of father you wanted and didn't get. You don't need to devote every moment to business. You have enough money to support a family and spend time with them. Didn't you ever wish your dad would spend more time with you?"

"I am not getting married or having children," he repeated firmly.

And he definitely wasn't sharing his feelings about his parents with her. He shared them with no one, not even his brother.

But for a flicker of a second he wondered what having children with Abrienda would be like. Laughing little boys or girls, happy, surrounded by love. Abrienda's children would be lucky in having her for a mother. He almost envied her future.

"Say it enough and maybe you'll convince yourself," she said.

"I don't need to convince myself, just you."

The bubble popped and he was back in the rain wishing Manuel would find them so they'd have a dry and warm place to sleep.

She laughed. "I hardly factor in to any equations in your life. But when I read in the newspaper that you are engaged, I shall send you a note to say I told you so."

"Why do you think I would marry?"

"Because I hate to think of waste," she said.

"What does that mean?"

"Think what you can contribute to the gene pool when you have kids."

Domingo didn't know whether to laugh or not. She was teasing him. He was fascinated by Abrienda's thought processes. She was pretty in a low-key way with no makeup. And the clothes she wore were more serviceable than stylish.

Still, there was something about her that had him looking

at her more and more. So far she hadn't presumed on any kind of friendship, though he could think of several others who would have already tried.

He liked talking with her, really talking, about things like her philosophies on marriage. What would the man be like to attract her attention and keep her with him all her life?

For the first time ever, Domingo felt the sting of regret for the way he foresaw his life unfolding.

"Getting cold?" he asked to squelch his thoughts.

"A little."

The rain had turned to drizzle and the wind had finally died down. But the temperature had fallen even more.

"It'll be totally dark soon, we might as well resign ourselves to sleeping in the basket and hoping the morning brings the sun," he said.

"So we just sleep here? With only two blankets and no room to stretch out?"

"Do you have an alternate place in mind?" he asked, trying to get comfortable around the propane tanks.

Listening to the rain for a moment, Abrienda knew there were no alternatives. She longed to hear the truck's horn alerting them it was almost upon them. Or at least catch a glimmer of headlights shining through the trees. Domingo had tried every half hour to raise someone and no one responded. They were truly on their own for the night.

Abrienda wasn't sure how she felt about that. In other circumstances, she might have been over the moon at the thought of spending the night with Domingo. But the longer she spent with him, the more she saw the difference between them. Would he be more inclined to see her as an available woman if she had her hair styled by some high-priced stylist and wore designer clothes?

Unlikely.

She wouldn't really want to base a relationship on such superficial artifice. She wanted to fall in love and find the happiness she remembered her parents sharing. What would it be like to be married to Domingo, to come home at the end of each day and prepare dinner together, talking over what they'd done since they'd last seen each other? Kissing between cutting vegetables and preparing the entrée? Discussing plans for a weekend or holiday? Really getting to know him and having him know her?

She longed for the kind of marriage that brought two people close, so they could essentially shut out the rest of the world and be happy together. Wouldn't it be even more special with Domingo? She closed her eyes and wished briefly for something that would never be. Then she made up her mind to enjoy their fleeting time together.

"So, what's the plan?" she asked.

Chapter Ten

"We'll put one of the blankets under us to protect us against heat loss as much as possible, then continue to share the second one together, capturing as much body heat as we can. At least the rain hasn't found its way inside."

Sleep together, that's what he was saying. Abrienda's thoughts raced. Sure, they'd both be fully clothed, but to sleep with Domingo? She wasn't sure she could do that.

What if during the night she gave herself away? What if he suspected the major crush she had on him? She'd be so embarrassed, she'd have to walk back to Barcelona, that's what.

Yet the awkward position made it unlikely that he'd guess her feelings for him. She'd practically been sitting in his lap all afternoon, so this would be more of the same. She knew they'd doze, but it was too uncomfortable for a deep sleep.

"If we each wrapped up in one blanket, that would cover all sides."

"You forgot the shared body heat," he reminded her.

"Oh, yeah, that."

She swallowed hard. So she wasn't the sophisticated kind of woman he normally saw. She could handle this. Camping wasn't like normal life, and the truth of the matter was that there was no risk.

Domingo argued with her, even seemed annoyed with her sometimes, but he'd given no indication he'd like to do more with her than the light banter he'd indulged in from time to time.

"Okay," she said, scooting out of the way so he could lay out the first blanket. Then he sat down, pulling the blanket up to his shoulders against the side of the basket. She wedged herself in between the floor and him, half on the blanket, half on Domingo. A moment later the other blanket covered them both.

It was warmer being next to Domingo.

"Relax," he said softly, shifting to put his arm around her and drawing her closer.

Abrienda couldn't relax. Every fiber of her being was attuned to him yet she dare not give way.

"I'm fine," she said.

"You're stiff as a board. I'm not going to bite."

She took a deep breath, which pressed her breasts against his arm. Letting it out in a gasp, she knew she'd never sleep tonight. Every nerve tingled. Her blood pounded in her veins. She was aware of every inch of his body touching hers.

He brushed his lips against her cheek.

"What are you doing?" She jerked up to stare at him.

"Trying to warm you up," he said, trailing kisses down her cheek.

She wiggled, but he didn't give an inch.

"This is *so* not a good idea," she said, her heart racing.

"Why is that?" he asked, between feather light kisses.

"We hardly know each other." Was her voice growing

breathless?

"So we get to know each other better. If you tally the hours we've put in, we've already spent more time together than I can remember spending with anyone else in years."

"All the more reason to remember where we are. This is a false environment. We move in different circles. After this race we'll probably only see each other on the rare occasions when you come to our offices."

She was babbling, but she couldn't stop. She tried to find every reason she could to keep her distance, when everything in her wanted to snuggle closer and feel the delight she knew Domingo would deliver.

"We're only trying to get some sleep here, Abrienda, not making a life commitment."

"I know that," she said sharply, wishing she could regally take one blanket and move as far from Domingo as she could go. Which wouldn't be far with the limited shelter they had. One step outside and she'd be soaked in no time. She'd already had to go out a couple of times and she didn't want to be wet going to sleep. If she could even sleep being so close to him.

"I'm not your type," she added.

"Do I have a type?" he asked, drawing her even closer.

Abrienda felt the length of him against her. Heat soared. She wouldn't be cold, at least. But she *was* totally wide-awake.

"Sophisticated, trendy, stylish."

She tried to focus on the conversation and not the sensations racing through her.

"But maybe that's because I hadn't met you," he said, brushing another kiss against her cheek, dangerously close to her lips.

She caught her breath, feeling the pounding of her heart. It rocked her. He had to feel it, too.

"Don't mess with me, Domingo," she warned.

"Call me Dom, my closest friends do. And they don't ever get as close as this," he said before his lips found hers and he kissed her the way he had the other night.

His hand threaded in her hair, holding her close as his mouth caused her to go into sensory overload. She was soaring higher and higher. In a split second she went from trying to push him away to turning to get as close as she could get, her own hands holding him tightly. It was glorious. Was forbidden fruit all the sweeter for being unattainable?

Time stood still. It might be dark outside but the kaleidoscope of colors in her mind lit up the night. The cold was left behind as heat spread to every inch. Engulfed in emotions, reveling in the exquisite sensations that roiled through her, she never wanted the moment to end. Forgotten was the weather and the tight quarters of the basket. She was soaring.

She didn't know how long they kissed, but when Domingo finally moved to her throat and the pulse point there, she tried to regain a modicum of control. His hands had moved from her head to her back, holding her close as they shared kiss after kiss. She felt she could conquer the world, if only he'd never let her go.

Finally the passion eased a bit and she could catch a random thought or two that reminded her they had no business doing this.

The chase team could arrive at any moment.

She had her brother to look after.

Domingo was an avowed bachelor and notorious playboy.

She was the head of her family and had responsibilities.

He felt the change in her at once and pulled back to look at her, trying to read her emotions in the dark.

"What's wrong?"

"Is this your way of trying to seduce me?' she asked breathlessly.

He'd do so in a heartbeat if he thought she was that kind of woman, but he knew she wasn't.

"No, it's my way of enjoying being with you. There is no seduction planned. This is hardly the setup for that."

"Darn," she said, surprising him.

"Unless you?"

"No. Never mind. This can't go anywhere."

"Because?"

"For tons of reasons, but mostly because I'm not the kind to do casual sex."

He hesitated a moment. If he tried hard, could he get her to change her mind?

No, he wouldn't do that. Abrienda was special.

"Then we stop now. But if you change your mind, you let me know, right?"

He could feel her smile.

"You'll be the first to know," she said, tucking her head in against his cheek. In a few moments he felt her relax.

If any of his friends saw him now they'd laugh their heads off. He was not going to push the issue, much as he longed to do so. Holding Abrienda, feeling her curled up against him, had him fantasizing about how fabulous it'd be to make love to her. If he pushed it, however, he ran the risk of alienating her totally. And that was not something he planned to ever do.

She'd already turned him down for a date when they returned to Barcelona. Now that was something he'd try to change her mind about. Let her get to know him better, let him get to know her and see where it might lead.

He could start with insisting she accompany him to the Barcelona Business Alliance to see her boss present him, or them, with the check. She deserved recognition for her part in the race.

He could picture her in a lovely burgundy gown, her cheeks tinged with pink, her eyes sparkling and happy. They would have dinner at the BBA meeting, but afterward, he'd take her dancing until the wee hours.

"Abrienda?"

He'd get her commitment now and have that date to look forward to.

She didn't answer. She'd already fallen asleep.

Domingo tucked the blanket around her and let himself relax toward sleep. He'd never spent the entire night with a woman before in such circumstances. Or with one who insisted they had nothing in common.

Yet in the morning they'd waken together after being bundled close all night. Would it change her outlook? Would she immediately think about how to capitalize on the situation?

Old habits kicked in. He needed to make sure his defenses were in place. Escorting her to an event or two didn't mean a life-long commitment. She had him feeling vaguely dissatisfied with his life, which was going just the way he wanted. Not for him a family, children, shared experiences, activities and one woman for life.

The rain stopped sometime in the night. When Domingo woke before dawn, he heard only silence. Easing himself away from Abrienda, he quickly tucked the blanket around her to keep her as warm as possible. He wanted to take a look outside. Finding a flashlight, he rose and stepped out.

The stars shone in the sky and all clouds had blown away. It was cool, but not too bad. Checking his watch, he saw dawn was still an hour away. Time they began to ready the balloon for liftoff as soon as it started growing light. If the envelope had not gotten wet. If it had, there was no telling how long they'd be stranded.

"Domingo?"

He heard Abrienda coming up to stand beside him.

"Is it time to go?"

"We'll wait for light. I want to check the envelope but need to wait for daylight to do that. With luck, it'll be mostly dry.

"Can two of us get it ready to fly?"

"Of course."

It wouldn't be easy, but he had to make it work. They couldn't afford the time to wait for other help. If Vincente got airborne before Domingo did, he could close the distance. Or maybe Vincente hadn't found shelter, either. Maybe his envelope had gotten wet and they could call a time-out or something until the balloons dried.

When dawn lightened the area enough, he went to the large tarp covering the balloon. The mound made sure the rain had run off, but it was where the envelope touched the ground he worried about. Had water seeped beneath the tarp?

Careful to lift the tarp so no water slid to the balloon, he was pleased to note the ground beneath was still dry. The makeshift ditch he'd carved out had done the job: the envelope was dry.

"Spread the tarp, dry side up, out this way. We'll roll the balloon out on it as far as we can to keep it dry."

In less than ten minutes Domingo fired up the fan using the auxiliary line from the propane tank to begin the inflation process. As the envelope filled, the top moved beyond the tarp and the plastic they'd also placed down. But not much of the envelope touched the ground. He hoped the light touch would keep it from absorbing mud and moisture.

Finally he fired the jets, and the envelope began to rise.

Once it cleared the ground, Abrienda quickly folded the tarp and plastic sheet and brought them to the basket which Domingo had set upright. Stepping in as if she'd done it all her life, she stowed them in the side pouches and glanced at Domingo.

"Will it fly?"

"Let's hope so."

It was taking longer to fill, and one spot near the top seemed darker. Whether it was damp or muddy, he didn't know. He hoped it was of a small enough size not to hamper lift.

Abrienda watched the balloon, keeping her gaze firmly away from Domingo. She felt awkward and unsure after last night. His kisses had been the stuff of dreams. Was he astute enough to realize the kisses she gave in return were full of feelings she had no business having for him?

Closing her eyes for a moment, she was swept back to those heady moments. She couldn't help the smile that tugged at her lips. Her heart yearned for more. Snapping open her eyes, she tried to ignore the clamoring feelings. Finding him already up when she'd awakened had helped and hurt. There'd been no lingering over a few kisses to get the day going.

By the time they were airborne, she hoped she'd regain her equilibrium. Nothing had happened. Except Abrienda had fallen a bit more for the man.

At least he didn't want to talk about it this morning. Then again, why would he? For him, she was the latest one in a long line of women he'd romanced.

Slowly the basket rocked, then moved as it lifted from the ground. Abrienda was used to feeling no speed or movement by now. Glancing at the horizon, she estimated they were rising quickly. The hot air was lighter than the colder air from the night.

She liked these times, she realized with surprise. Unable to tell how high they were, she didn't feel quite as nervous.

Domingo took the binoculars and scanned the sky. He paused a moment, and then gestured to Abrienda.

"Vincente is also getting an early start. Can you see his balloon over there?"

She looked in the direction he pointed. "Can he catch us?"

"Not likely as long as we stay up. But we don't have full tanks. We'll have to set down and replenish before long."

The radio crackled. Manuel came through and Domingo quickly answered.

"That's the plan," he concluded a short time later.

If the balloon continued in the current direction, they'd

find a small town before long. The chase team was racing there in hope of finding a field for the balloon so they could exchange tanks. They'd spent most of the night trying to find Domingo.

"Will our stopping give Vincente the edge?"

"Depends on if his chase team was able to get him full tanks yesterday," Domingo said.

Abrienda exchanged places with him and looked at the distant balloon. She hoped Vincente needed fuel as much as they did. She wanted to keep their lead and maybe lengthen it.

He'd made her angry ordering her to participate. Now allegiance had been changed. She was crew for Domingo Ortego and she would do all she could for this team to win.

She carefully turned around to watch the direction the balloon was traveling. In the distance she saw some rooftops. As they drifted closer, buildings in the town became visible.

Manuel had found a soccer field on the map and that's what Domingo was heading for. They weren't very high, so she hoped they could line up with the soccer field and land there with no trouble.

It was on the far side of town. When Domingo spotted it he began his descent. The field was to the left, how was he going to get the balloon to change course?

Abrienda watched. Caught up with trying to will the balloon to land in the field, she forgot to be afraid. Amazingly, Domingo landed right on the edge. As the balloon began to collapse, he fed it enough heat to keep it upright. The grass was glittering with raindrops.

"You did it!" she exclaimed.

Excited, she threw her arms around him. He caught her

up and turned her around in the narrow basket, ending with a kiss on her mouth.

"We need to get the ropes in place," he said, uncoiling them and quickly tying them to the basket cleats.

Abrienda knew the routine and, using the step, quickly went over the side and was already looking for something to tether to. The grassy field offered nothing.

She told Domingo. He looked over the side and scanned the field.

"We're okay for now. When the truck gets here, we'll have stakes we can use."

Who knew how long it would be before the ground team arrived?

Somewhere along the way something had changed. Had it been her? She wanted to spend time with Domingo now instead of avoiding him. She wasn't getting in over her head, she told herself. A few kisses, however passionate, meant nothing.

The radio crackled. Domingo got it and responded. The team wasn't far away.

Abrienda watched expectantly in the direction of the village. It'd be good to get a hot meal and freshen up a bit before heading out again. She scanned the sky. No sign of her boss's balloon. Was he still moving or had he set down to refuel?

Once the chase truck came into view, things moved swiftly. Julio took Domingo and Abrienda into town for some much-needed hot food. The others examined the balloon, checked all the ropes and connections, exchanged the tanks, pounded stakes into the ground to hold the tether ropes and, using the wind direction, tried to calculate where a good spot for landing would be for the next refill.

"No time for a room and shower," Domingo said as they reached the outskirts of the town. "Just a hot meal and time to wash and change clothes if you want."

"I do," Abrienda said, grateful for that much at least.

One hour later they were back at the field. In the distance, Vincente Alvarez's balloon was drifting by, a mile or more toward the west.

"He didn't stop," Abrienda said.

"Apparently not. Ready to go?" Domingo asked the ground crew.

"He won't get ahead, will he?" she asked.

"Depends. Let's get up and going."

For the first time Abrienda shared the excitement of the team, racing to get airborne again, hoping they could beat the other balloon. She watched as they rose from the ground, trying to figure out how far ahead Vincente might be and if they had a hope of catching up.

"Relax, we're loaded with fuel and will go as long as we can. Even if he filled up last night, he'll have to come down before us and we'll sail by. You can wave if you wish," he teased.

She laughed, feeling giddy with happiness. From stark fear to delight, she'd come a long way in a few days. Primarily because of Domingo.

"Of course. And may the best team win—us."

After the previous day and the storm, this day was clear and cooler, perfect for ballooning. The wind at the higher elevations was still brisk and when she ventured to look out,

Abrienda could tell they were moving faster than earlier in the race.

"This is fun," she said in surprise a little later. If she didn't look down, it was. She felt carefree and happy. And when she looked at Domingo and saw the gleam of interest in his eyes, she felt very feminine.

"You shouldn't be so surprised, why do you think so many people enjoy the sport? So maybe I'm not the big, bad guy for taking you from your home one morning?" he said whimsically.

She grinned at him. "Maybe not."

He laughed and she caught her breath. He had a day or two's growth of beard. His hair was not the neat cut she was used to seeing in the office, but tousled and windblown, and she wanted so much to run her fingers through it. To have the right to do that.

Looking away lest she reveal her thoughts, she watched as the other balloon also sailed silently on the wind.

"If the wind holds and keeps in this direction, we'll be close to another town when we stop tonight. We'll definitely get rooms and a good hot meal," Domingo said a short time after he'd made some calculations on the map.

"I'll look forward to that."

But she would miss the enforced intimacy they'd enjoyed last night. She'd never have an occasion to spend the night with Domingo again.

The thought put a damper on her delight. Every moment she spent learning about him was bittersweet. She relished the knowledge and the change in her viewpoint about him. But each moment also meant that the end of the race was that much closer. The end of their time together.

Next week she'd be back at work. The next time she saw Domingo Ortego he'd be in the society section of the newspaper with some gorgeous woman accompanying him.

It was almost dusk when Domingo put the balloon down on a grassy meadow near the town of Santa Maria de las Montañas.

Abrienda had been quiet during the afternoon and he wondered what she was thinking. Last night had been unexpected in many ways. Not the least was the way it changed how he saw her.

She continued to intrigue him, primarily because she was so noticeably different from the women he normally associated with. He couldn't imagine his own mother taking last night in stride, much less the younger women he saw socially.

He wondered how she would fit into his social schedule. First the BBA dinner, then maybe a weekend in Madrid? The shopping there was amazing. Women were always telling him that. Would she like to sail the Med while the good weather continued? If he asked Jose to go, he knew she'd agree.

That was the key, to make sure that he included her brother some of the time, until she grew used to seeing him.

He'd start with the sailing, and work his way up to a weekend away together.

It was late by the time everyone reached the accommodations for the night, a small hotel in the center of Santa Maria.

Once again Abrienda had her own room, and as soon as she got her key, she headed for the elevator. Jose had left for his school trip, so there was no one to call. But the thought of a hot bath and then a comfortable bed held amazing appeal.

"Abrienda." Domingo caught up with her at the elevator. The others were still by the front desk.

"Have dinner with me," he said.

"Aren't you tired of my company by now?" she asked, her heart fluttering.

He didn't have to spend his time away from the balloon with her.

"No. We can eat in my suite if you like and not have the bother of others around."

Her heart kicked into overdrive. Dinner alone in his suite? *Just* dinner?

"You don't want to discuss the race with the others?" she said, stalling.

Dare she take this chance?

"Not tonight. Maria and Manuel are plotting our most likely route for tomorrow. Tonight will be just for us."

"What time?" she asked, still uncertain.

"Say, eight?"

The elevator arrived, its doors opening.

"What room?" she asked, stepping inside.

He remained in the lobby.

"Six eleven."

"See you at eight," she said as the doors slid shut.

Reaching her room, she quickly unpacked her nicest top and jeans. She had nothing suitable for a date with one of Barcelona's most eligible bachelors, but then, she reasoned, he'd hardly be dressed up himself.

The room was spacious, with a small sitting area near the

window and a huge bed dominating one wall. The ensuite bathroom contained a spa tub and a large shower. While not as luxurious as the one she'd had that first night, it was still more than she was used to. And it beat sleeping in the rain by a mile.

Her shower was quick, hot and delightful. With clean hair brushed until it gleamed, a light application of makeup and a freshly pressed cranberry-red top, she felt like a new woman.

Staring at her reflection in the mirror she tried to look sophisticated and cool. Instead, her eyes sparkled and her cheeks were flushed with color in anticipation of spending a portion of the evening with Domingo. And that was all. Dinner, some conversation and then she'd say good-night.

Just before eight there was a knock on her door. Opening it, Abrienda saw Domingo standing there. He'd shaved, combed his hair and put on a dark shirt with dark slacks. With his tanned skin and dark eyes, he looked sexy and dangerous.

"I usually pick up my dates for the evening," he said lazily.

His gaze traveled from her head to her toes and back up again.

"You clean up nicely," he said, flashing a smile that threatened Abrienda's good sense.

"Thank you, I might say the same."

"I looked like a pirate or something until I shaved," he said.

Maybe she had a thing for pirates, she thought he'd looked incredible. Even better now.

"I'm ready. Let me get my room key," she said, retrieving it from the dresser.

"I could have made it to your room safely," she said as

they took the elevator up two floors.

"I'm sure, but this is better," he said.

When they entered the suite, Abrienda glanced around. It was as luxurious as hers had been that first night. Domingo obviously liked traveling first class. What would that be like, she wondered. Far better not to get too used to it. This was so temporary.

Dinner was delivered by room service minutes later. She stood by the window looking at the lights of the small town as the waiter set up their table.

"Very pretty," she said.

Turning, she looked at the feast Domingo had ordered. It seemed like enough food to feed the entire crew.

"I hope you like veal," he said.

"I do."

Crossing to the table as the waiter prepared to place the first course in front of them, she felt like a princess or something. Usually she and Jose ate in the kitchen of their small apartment.

"Lovely," she said.

Domingo poured cider into the glasses and raised his in toast.

"To our successful completion of the race."

"To winning," she replied touching her glass to his.

Once the waiter had been assured everything was to their liking, he withdrew.

"Alone at last," Domingo said.

Abrienda laughed nervously.

"We are alone together all day."

"But here we have nothing to do but concentrate on each

other."

She sipped her sparkling beverage wondering what he meant by that.

"And the delicious dinner," she said.

"True. We have the evening ahead of us."

"Actually, not a long one if we are getting up at five in the morning," she said, tasting the veal.

It almost melted in her mouth it was so tender.

Abrienda had no need to worry about conversation while they ate; Domingo was a skilled conversationalist and she enjoyed the banter they exchanged.

After the crème brûlée dessert, he suggested they move to the sofa for after-dinner coffee.

"That'll keep me up forever," she said. "But I won't say no to a little."

He dimmed the lights and poured the hot coffee.

Abrienda's heart pounded like a drum. Was this a setup for seduction? She'd love some more kisses from the man, but knew her limitations. She wasn't getting intimately involved with Domingo Ortego. The minute he returned to Barcelona, she'd be but a minuscule memory in his mind as he escorted some of the city's most glamorous women around.

"Did you call your brother?" he asked, sitting beside her on the sofa and lifting his coffee cup in salute.

"Jose is on his school trip. He left this morning."

"Gone for how long?"

"Several days. He's one of the few students chosen for this trip. I know he'll have a million things to tell me when I'm back home."

"You'll have things to tell him, as well," Domingo said.

She took a sip of the coffee feeling its warmth spread. She didn't plan to tell her brother everything.

The unexpected ring of the telephone startled Abrienda and she jumped a bit.

Domingo rose and crossed the room to answer it.

"Helena, where are you?" he asked. Listening for a moment, he slowly smiled. "Sorry to hear that. Sounds like you are close enough to have come into Santa Maria."

Abrienda glanced at her watch. It was getting late. She needed to get to sleep if she was getting up early again. Placing her cup back on the saucer, she rose. Crossing to the window, she tried to ignore the conversation behind her. It sounded as if Helena were reporting in to Domingo, and wasn't happy with where they were staying.

When he hung up, Abrienda turned and raised her eyebrows in silent question.

"Your boss stopped for the night a few miles from here. There's cell service, but no hotels. Helena said after last night in the rain and tonight in a camping environment again, I owe her big time."

Abrienda grinned and nodded.

"I'm sure she feels that way. While I'm living in the lap of luxury."

He crossed to her and brushed back her hair.

"You look good in the lap of luxury," he said, and lowered his face to hers, his lips closing over hers.

Magical kisses were another perk of the race. Abrienda reached up to encircle his neck when Domingo pulled her closer. Body pressed to body, mouth pressed to mouth, he deepened the kiss and Abrienda responded like a flower to the sun. Desire rose. Time stood still.

His hands caressed her back, holding her against him as every nerve ending in her body craved a closer contact. This was the man who had practically kidnapped her for the race. Who'd opened up to her as she'd never expected. He'd been honest and forthright about not expecting anything more than a fling before moving on to another woman. He wasn't for marriage and children and growing old together.

But she was.

Regretfully, she pulled back and looked at him. Domingo rested his forehead on hers and gazed into her eyes. She was pleased to see he was breathing as hard as she was.

"I can't do this," she whispered.

"You seem to do it very well," he said softly.

"We have four more days of the race, then you'll go back to your life and I will go back to mine. We have nothing in common."

"It's just a few kisses," he said. "And we don't have to part after the race. I want you to come with me to the BBA dinner, when I accept your boss's check. You're helping me to win, so you should share the limelight."

"Don't count your chickens," she warned.

He laughed.

"We will win. And Vincente will hate giving me that check."

"And am I part of the prize? Do you plan to lure his PA away from him?"

Domingo straightened and let her go.

"If you think that of me, you don't know me at all. I have an excellent PA and I'm not looking for another."

Abrienda felt suddenly cold when he stepped back. She should guard her tongue. She'd only been teasing.

"I know. I'm sorry."

He relaxed. "No, I'm sure I overreacted. Say you'll go with me to the BBA dinner."

She considered and then nodded.

"If we win, I'll go with you."

"We *will* win," he said again, absolutely sure of himself.

"Thank you for dinner," she said, walking to the door.

He was there when she reached it.

"I'll escort you back to your room if you insist on returning there now," he said.

She regretted her hasty words about him luring her away from Vincente, as they had shattered the moment. Still better, perhaps, to end any fantasies she had before she got in too deep. Fairy tales were well and good for children, but they weren't for women who had responsibilities.

Chapter Eleven

Abrienda had a quick breakfast in her room the next morning. She'd had trouble sleeping during the night and had woken early enough to indulge herself. When she joined the others in the lobby, her eyes went straight to Domingo. He'd obviously had no trouble sleeping during the night as he looked as fresh as ever. Looking at him had her catching her breath.

When was she going to get over this stupid feeling? He was just another man. Granted more gorgeous than most she knew, but just a man.

Maria came down last and hurried over to the group.

"Sorry I'm late. I had the worst time getting up this morning."

Domingo glanced at Abrienda. "No such trouble with you, I take it."

"I'm here, aren't I?"

When they piled into the truck, Abrienda was pressed against Domingo. Had he deliberately arranged the seating? She looked straight ahead, not seeing much in the dark, and feeling every inch of him pressed against her.

They lifted off at dawn. Domingo kept to himself. Abrienda still regretted her hasty outburst last night, but she'd been scared of the feelings for him that grew each day. She didn't want to be attracted to him. Didn't want to admire him or feel he was becoming special to her. But a person didn't necessarily have control over the way they felt, just the way they acted. It'd be better if they kept a professional relationship. It would be easier for her to get over her feelings for him when they returned home.

"If we maintain our lead today, I think we'll be home free," Domingo said later in the morning, looking back at Vincente's balloon.

Abrienda stood up and looked behind them. She couldn't judge distances, but from the small size of the balloon, the others were several miles behind.

"Good," she said.

She wasn't feeling charitable toward her boss right now. He'd put her in this situation. She'd have been much better off not spending so much time with Domingo. Yet how could she regret even one second of it? When else in her life would she have such an adventure?

"The next BBA dinner meeting is in two weeks," Domingo said.

So he *had* meant what he said when he'd invited her as his date. She looked at him.

"I'll be delighted to attend," she said formally.

She'd have to blow a week's salary on a suitable dress, but it would be worth it for one more evening in his company.

"Good," he said, looking satisfied.

Gradually they regained the camaraderie that had blossomed over the last few days and the time passed swiftly. They set down with the team waiting, and only thirty minutes later they were aloft again.

Through the afternoon they gained even more distance on Vincente's balloon. The storm had made the difference. Now they just had to maintain the gap between them and they'd win easily.

As shadows on the ground grew longer, Domingo began searching for a place to put down. He ended up in a large field about a half hour's drive from a town behind them. Debating whether to camp out or seek a room in town, Domingo decided to go for town. They had a substantial lead and could afford the travel time to and from a hotel. He smiled when Maria danced in place.

"She's not much of a camper," he said to the group in general. The others gently teased her but Maria was made of strong stuff. She merely laughed and said the others could thank her when they got a good night's sleep.

To Abrienda's surprise, when they reached town, Vincente and his group were already in the hotel Domingo chose. Of course the men had similar tastes in hotels, so that should be no surprise. What did astonish her was the fact that there were a couple of newspaper reporters interviewing Vincente.

"Where does he find them?" she murmured on their way to the registration desk. Domingo had his hand at the small of her back, and merely glanced over to the group congregated near the windows.

"He must have the best PR firm in the country," he murmured back.

Domingo checked them all in and turned to watch Vincente pontificate on his strategy for winning, despite being behind. He caught Domingo's eye and turned away quickly, making sure the reporters stayed with him and didn't go to Domingo for his side of the story.

"You should go tell them how far ahead we are," Abrienda said as she watched.

"He knows," Domingo said.

"But the reporters don't."

"They will at the finish. That's all that counts."

As their group headed for the elevators, Helena crossed the lobby quickly, calling after Domingo.

"I need to talk to you," she said when she caught up, tugging him to one side.

Their conversation was hurried and quiet. Abrienda wondered what emergency could have arisen to get his PA so upset. From what she'd seen of Helena, the woman was used to dealing with difficult men and trying situations. She wouldn't be easily upset.

Though dealing with Vincente Alvarez could sometimes be extremely trying, as Abrienda well knew.

An elevator arrived as Manuel was sorting out their bags. Abrienda reached for hers just as the doors opened and Teresa Valquez stepped out.

Abrienda stared in disbelief. What was she doing here? How had she known they would be staying at this hotel? Turning slightly, Abrienda sought Domingo. He and Helena were still talking.

"Domingo," Teresa called gaily.

Abrienda watched as he looked up and saw Teresa. There was no expression on his face. Helena had obviously already warned him.

The reporters turned and watched as the pretty blonde ran across the room and flung herself against Domingo. He caught her, and Abrienda watched in dismay as she kissed him. He didn't seem to be protesting at all.

The pangs of jealousy and hurt hit her hard. She tried to tell herself she'd known all along nothing good would come of spending so much time with Domingo. But the reality still stung. She had thought—

Taking a breath, she pasted a smile on her face and started for the elevators.

She could hear the reporters behind her as they swarmed across the lobby and began to question Domingo.

Maria joined her in the elevator as they scooted in just before the doors closed.

"I'm on floor five," she said.

Abrienda looked at her room key. "Me, too."

"As soon as I get to my room I'm calling Helena to get the story about the miraculous appearance of Ms. Valquez. I bet Domingo is fit to be tied."

"Why?" Abrienda looked at Maria. "I thought they were dating."

"Maybe." Maria shrugged. "But she was a pain from the get-go at the festival. You saw how she showed up that first day. Racing is serious to Domingo, and all she wanted was his total attention. Like that would happen."

"I think my boss was hoping for that," Abrienda said, longing to ask more, but afraid of hearing the answers.

"Sure, if Domingo could be distracted, Alvarez had a better shot at winning. But that'll never happen. You know that. He's so focused."

Abrienda nodded, remembering the picture she'd seen on the Internet with Domingo and Teresa attending some reception. He'd looked pretty focused on *her* that night.

"See you at eight," Maria said as the elevator reached their floor. Domingo had told the team they'd meet for dinner then.

"Okay," Abrienda said. She didn't want to spend the evening with the crew, trying to pretend everything was fine when she thought her heart was nicked a bit. But she liked even less the idea that in boycotting the meal she might give the impression that Teresa's arrival had somehow caused a problem.

She'd *known* nothing would come of Domingo's attention. So why did it hurt that his flamboyant girlfriend had shown up? She didn't expect more kisses from him and another night dining alone together, or the prospect of spending hours in his arms as she had in the storm.

Abrienda went on a few more doors and reached her room. She was glad Domingo had arranged for each of them to have a private room. She was relieved not to have to share with anyone tonight.

Domingo watched as Abrienda and Maria entered the elevator. He'd give her a minute to get to her room and then call her.

"You're ahead of Alvarez. That is fabulous," Teresa said, still clinging to his arm. Smiling prettily for the reporters, she made sure of her hold on him.

He pulled away and frowned.

"I asked what you were doing here, Teresa."

He ignored the men with notebooks and looked at her.

"Alvarez called me and said his little secretary wasn't

doing well on the balloon and would I consider returning. I've missed you. Now I can continue the race with you and the secretary can return home. It worked out perfectly. He said he'd make sure I got a ride from here to your balloon no matter where you set down tonight. Aren't you the tiniest bit happy to see me?"

"You made your position clear. We have nothing further to talk about," he muttered.

Checking to make sure everyone had their rooms assigned, he lifted his bag and headed for the elevators. Teresa walked right beside him.

"I think it was nice of her boss to think of her welfare," Teresa said.

"Maybe." Domingo knew what Teresa was saying was probably true.

Abrienda hated being in the air. He'd seen her pale in fear, grow sick in fright. Had she gone behind his back and asked her boss to help her out?

Probably, since being altruistically concerned for one of his employees didn't sound very much like Alvarez.

"So…I am on the fifth floor," Teresa said in her sultry voice.

Domingo merely looked at her.

"Where is your room?" she asked when he didn't volunteer the information.

"On one of the upper floors."

"I could go with you and wait while you change for dinner," she suggested.

"I'm meeting everyone in the lobby at eight. We'll decide where to eat then," he said, quickly changing his plans. His original thought had been to see if Abrienda wanted another quiet dinner together. No way would he substitute Teresa for Abrienda.

When he reached his room, sans Teresa, he tossed his bag on the bed and went to the phone asking for Abrienda's room. The phone rang several times before he hung up. Was she already in the shower? Probably.

Once he finished his own shower and had shaved again, he tried her room once more. This time the line was busy. Domingo hung up feeling frustrated. Glancing at his watch, he noted it was close to eight. If he didn't make arrangements before then, she'd be downstairs with everyone else and he'd lose his chance to have dinner alone with her.

It was two minutes to eight when Domingo gave up trying to reach Abrienda and headed downstairs.

The crew was congregated near the big glass doors leading outside. Teresa was flirting with Manuel. Maria and Abrienda stood on the outskirts talking. Julio and Paolo were watching Teresa.

Most people watched her, Domingo thought. She always looked stunning, and she did tonight in that clinging dress. She looked ready for dinner, and the rest of the crew looked as if they should be mopping floors somewhere. He was dressed as they were. Teresa was the one out of place.

Dinner at a nearby restaurant proved disastrous. Teresa sat right beside him and spoke to no one else. The crew tried to carry on a conversation about the race, how far they were ahead and the chances of Alvarez conceding before the last day.

Every time, Teresa tuned out their discussion and tried to

engage him in an intimate topic excluding the rest.

Abrienda watched them, her expression obviously one of disdain. Domingo had to admit that in comparing the two women, it was Teresa who came up short. She liked to go out to expensive restaurants or clubs and be seen. One of her favorite aspects was showing off her new clothes and her escort. Flirting came naturally to her and she didn't limit herself to her date.

In the past that had been a normal date for him.

Tonight he'd much rather sit beside Abrienda and engage her in conversation. Listen to her views on things and have the give and take that normally only came with longtime friends. Ones who didn't feel the need to impress him.

With Abrienda he was uncertain if she even liked him.

And he wanted her to. For the first time he could remember, he cared what a woman thought about him. He was growing more and more fascinated with her. He'd like to explore all the avenues open to them. To take her back to her room and kiss her good-night. To share breakfast in the morning. He looked forward to their time alone in the gondola and felt she was opening up to him more and more each day. Wasn't that a good sign?

He had a sinking feeling that was not necessarily so.

"So if you are so far ahead, you don't need to push tomorrow, do you?" Teresa asked at one point, again changing the topic of discussion.

"It's always best to increase the lead," Domingo said. "Abrienda and I have worked hard to gain the advantage. There's no telling what might happen to slow us down at some future time, so the wider the lead, the better."

Teresa smiled at Abrienda.

"And you so afraid of heights. I think it's a real shame to coerce you into participating. I have no such fears." She turned back to Domingo. "We did well at the festival, didn't we?"

He shrugged, not wanting to dwell on how inappropriately she had dressed and behaved. Nor relive the constant complaints.

Manuel laughed.

"You could have done better," he said bluntly.

Teresa flashed her biggest smile at him, but anger shone in her eyes.

Abrienda watched, interested to see the interaction between Domingo and Teresa. It surprised her how much the rest of the crew disliked the other woman. There was nothing overt, but they didn't include her in the planning, didn't answer some of her questions, acting as if they hadn't heard. And each covered for the other. She looked at Domingo. Had he noticed?

She was flustered to find his gazed fixed on her.

"Abrienda is to be commended for doing so well despite her fear."

He raised his glass in silent toast.

She inclined her head slightly and made an effort not to glance at Teresa. She knew the woman would be furious, but so what? She felt on top of the world with Domingo's compliment.

Once dinner ended, Maria and Abrienda excused themselves and headed back to the hotel.

"I'm not going to oversleep tomorrow," Maria declared

as they bade the others good-night.

Domingo stood when they did, but made no move to detain them. Abrienda wished he had. She'd have stayed longer if he'd only asked. If she could have outlasted Teresa, the two of them might have had some quiet time together.

Which was silly, they had all day tomorrow to spend alone together. She knew she was hoarding the memories like a miser hoarded gold. Each one sparkling and special to her. At night, alone, her imagination soared. Sometimes she thought he looked at her in a particular way that suggested he was interested in her. She knew she was falling for him and was determined not to give way. Heartache was not something she wanted.

The walk back to the hotel was accomplished quickly. When they entered the lobby of the hotel, Helena was sitting in one of the chairs, reading a book. She glanced up and smiled when she saw Abrienda and Maria.

"How's it going?" she called.

"I'm still alive," Abrienda said, walking over to the other woman.

Maria continued to the elevator, calling out a good-night.

Abrienda sat beside Helena. "How about you?"

For a moment Helena said nothing, then shrugged.

"I don't envy you your job. I suspect your boss is a difficult man to work for."

"I've managed for the past three years."

"Then you are to be commended. Dom is much easier to deal with."

"I wouldn't have thought so," Abrienda said. "He's pretty driven to succeed."

Still, he had shown a different side to his personality on the trip. He was more caring than most people thought.

"But not by trampling over the feelings of others. Vincente Alvarez is a driving power and I believe an egomaniac," Helena said.

Abrienda laughed. Her boss did like to be the center of attention. Most of the time she didn't mind. She was content in her job. Until she could afford to move on.

"Are you waiting to see Domingo?" Abrienda asked.

"No, I just wanted some quiet time to read. My roommate insists on talking on the phone until she's too tired to continue. She has an endless supply of friends."

"Domingo allocated us to individual rooms," Abrienda said.

"Figures. He always does things top class. I think your boss is a penny-pincher. We're to get our own meals on this trip. But doubling up on rooms, when we find a hotel, is a pretty good way to short change the crew. I guess I'm lucky I don't have to pay for the room."

"How did he know we'd be here tonight?" she asked.

"A lucky guess on his part. We spend a lot of time in the balloon calculating rate of speed, direction, where we'll put down. He then has the ground crew radio ahead to any reporters who might be keeping tabs on the race. While it's not the Grand Prix, he's keeping the news alive in the Barcelona papers. I think he figures Teresa will be enough of a distraction to slow Domingo down, which shows he doesn't know my boss very well. Domingo's perfectly capable of separating work from play, and this race is too important to throw away at this point for some woman."

"Why is it so important to him to win?" Abrienda asked softly.

"Did you ask Domingo?" Helena asked.

Abrienda shrugged. "Once. He just said he wanted to show Vincente he wasn't the only one who could win at something."

"I probably should let him tell you. But it might help to know that Vincente pulled an underhanded deal about five years ago. It caused Domingo a huge monetary loss and damaged his reputation slightly. Things have been smoothed over since, and I'm sure Vincente has no idea Domingo still broods on that. This is merely one way to retaliate. And no one will ever know why, but I think it'll soothe Domingo's ire a bit. Winning means a lot, but it's having Vincente present the check at the BBA, that's the big thing. I think it'll take the sting out of the past a bit."

Abrienda wondered how Domingo could still deal with her boss if he had been underhanded. Domingo had a strong sense of integrity and honor.

"I'll let you keep reading," Abrienda said, rising. "See you at the finish."

Helena bade her good-night and returned to her book.

Upon reaching her room, Abrienda called the front desk to leave a wake-up call, then prepared for bed. She'd take a clue from Maria and get to bed early to waken refreshed. She was tired.

And disappointed Teresa had found them. If she hadn't, would Domingo have wanted to spend more time alone with her as he had before?

The sun woke Abrienda when its rays fell in her face. She

frowned and rolled over, opening her eyes. She sat up in panic. It was full daylight! She checked the clock; it was after seven. Good grief, what had happened to her wake-up call? She dashed from bed and dressed in record time. Domingo would have a fit.

Suddenly she stopped. Had he changed the departure time? If not, surely he'd have been pounding on her door by this time. There had been some talk last night about leaving later due to their lead, but she was sure she remembered him saying that he wanted to increase the lead, not tempt fate.

She finished dressing, then called Maria's room. No answer.

Packing her things, she left for the lobby. She'd be so embarrassed if everyone was waiting for her.

The lobby was empty. She went to the double doors leading to the street. No truck, no crew. No Domingo. Her trepidation increased. What was going on?

Turning, Abrienda entered the lobby and approached the registration desk. "Did the balloon crew leave already?" she asked.

"I believe both groups left before six," the desk clerk said. He frowned and asked, "Were you supposed to go with them?"

"Yes. And I left a wake-up call for four-thirty. It never came."

She couldn't have slept through the loud ring of the phone. How could they have left her? Was one of the crew already on the way back to get her?

The clerk frowned and clicked a few keys on the computer.

"Ah, that call was canceled shortly before midnight," he said.

"*I* didn't cancel it."

He frowned and clicked a few more keys. "I don't have the information on who canceled it, just that it was canceled. I apologize if that was in error."

She verified it was the call for her room, then turned, puzzled. Who would have canceled her wake-up call, and why hadn't Domingo come pounding on her door when she hadn't appeared with the rest of the crew?

"I don't understand. I'm part of the crew on that balloon. How could they leave me?"

"I'm sure I don't know, miss."

Abrienda turned away. What was she going to do? She had no idea why they would have left her. Surely there was a logical explanation. Maybe Domingo was letting her sleep in and Manuel or Maria would be back to get her and she'd find the balloon was already inflated by the time she reached it?

She turned back. "Is there a message for me?"

"Let me check." He turned and looked into the box on the back wall that had her room number. "Indeed, there is."

He handed her an envelope.

She crossed to the chairs where Helena had been reading the night before and sat to open the envelope.

"Your boss is a dear. Vincente suggested I take your place on Domingo's balloon so you can return home. No more fear of heights."

It was signed with Teresa's flamboyant signature.

Abrienda stared at the paper. She didn't believe it. Domingo had taken Teresa and left her behind.

"What did you think, you stupid woman," she muttered. "That he'd favor you over the woman he's been seeing the last few months?"

She'd thought he'd liked her. Their discussions had grown more and more personal. She'd learned more about him than anyone else she knew. She'd revealed some of her uncertainties raising Jose, and her future, as she had never done before.

She thought they were growing close.

But it had obviously only been on her side.

She'd been falling in love, hoping against hope that he'd been feeling some kind of special attachment for her. But this—it proved the race was the only thing he was interested in. Now he had a willing passenger and Abrienda was just so much excess baggage.

The enormity of the situation rose. She had virtually no money with her, no transportation, no brother at home to call on for help. She was truly stuck in this small town hundreds of miles from any place familiar. Just how was she going to get home?

Anger flared. How dare he bully her from her home, insist she accompany him when she was scared to death half the time, and then dump her the minute someone else showed up. He'd assured her she'd get home safely. If he didn't want her on the trip, it was up to him to arrange transportation home.

Thankfully she hadn't yet checked out. She returned to her room and headed for the phone. She called her office. The temp who'd replaced her for the length of the race answered. Abrienda asked for the number of Domingo's company.

She phoned there and talked to three different people, her

ire rising at each brush-off. Finally she asked for Philipe. She remembered his name from a comment Domingo made to Helena.

"Can I help you?" a masculine voice asked a moment later.

Abrienda took a deep breath. It was not this person's fault his boss was a jerk.

"This is Abrienda Delmarico. Domingo has stranded me in some little town up near the French border and I need to get back to Barcelona."

"I'm sorry, who did you say you were?"

"The woman he practically *kidnapped* to go on this stupid balloon race and then stranded with no way to get home. There might be some reporters still around who would love to hear that story," she finished.

That thought just occurred to her. Would they have left when her boss did? Or could she find one or two around to tell of the predicament Domingo had put her in? All sorts of fantasies played in her mind, but mostly she wanted to get home and put this behind her.

How dumb could one person be? A man like Domingo Ortego would never truly fall in love with someone like her. She was a novelty. Someone so different from women he knew, he was temporarily intrigued. But that interest had vanished. Winning the race trumped everything else.

She could call the papers herself for that matter. Not that it would get her home. She was so angry.

And disappointed.

And hurt.

She'd thought there was at least a tentative friendship developing. Did he think she willy-nilly kissed every man she spent some time with like she'd kissed him?

"I'm sorry, I don't recognize your name. I can get in touch with Domingo and get back to you," he said.

"Grrr."

She hung up the phone and called her office again.

"This is Abrienda, let me speak to Henrico, please."

In a roundabout way it was her boss's fault she was in this predicament. She'd get home at the company's expense and let Vincente sort out the costs with Domingo later.

Domingo gazed in the direction they were moving. Teresa stood at the side, watching their shadow cross the earth. Her perfume was cloying. Why she even wore it on a balloon was beyond him.

Firing up the jets again, he tried to quell his anger and, truth be known, his disappointment. He'd known from the beginning Abrienda had been afraid of heights. That she hadn't wanted to make the trip. Still, the last few days she'd seemed to do fine on the flights. And the conversations they'd had held a lot of appeal to him.

Yet she had jumped at the offer of letting Teresa substitute for her when she'd arrived at the hotel last night.

He'd been furious when he arrived at the truck that morning and seen Teresa there instead of Abrienda. He'd been on the point of going to her room and getting her when Teresa said Abrienda had asked to switch.

To double check, he'd asked the desk clerk to see if there was any message from Abrienda. There had been none. So then he'd checked to see if she'd left a wake-up call for this morning. The clerk had confirmed one had been placed, but then canceled later in the evening.

Probably after she'd spoken to Teresa.

He vented his anger with the burners, firing them up for longer than the normal ten seconds. The balloon rose. He wished he could rise above the surprising letdown he was feeling from Abrienda's defection.

At least Teresa appeared to be trying this time. She'd been the perfect passenger, except for the perfume. And the skintight T-shirt she wore. Her jacket opened to reveal as much as she could and still keep warm.

He was annoyed. Things had been going well and with the lead he had, he'd easily beat Vincente Alvarez.

But he'd pictured a totally different ending. He and Abrienda celebrating at the finish. Riding home together with the crew. Sharing in the glory of winning. Him taking her out for a quiet celebration, just the two of them.

Her brother would still have been on his trip, so perhaps she'd have invited him in. If she had, he'd have definitely accepted. Together they'd attend the BBA dinner. Together they could have received the check from her boss.

He could have told her then how much he wanted to beat Vincente Alvarez and why. She'd have understood.

The fantasy ended. The dinner was still on, but the ride home would certainly be different.

"I can hardly see Alvarez's balloon," Teresa said smugly. "He's so far behind, he hasn't a chance to win."

Domingo nodded and fired up the burners. The noise gave a rest to Teresa's constant chatter. The morning was not soothing like other days had been. Abrienda didn't speak a lot. He hadn't realized how much he'd enjoyed the silence, relished the challenge.

Today he was just irritated.

Abrienda could have at least told him to his face that she

didn't want to continue now that Teresa had arrived. He felt his anger rise. A courtesy call would have been nice. No, she should have verified with him whether the change was acceptable or not. Just because she wanted her own way didn't mean she got it. He wanted *her* on this flight.

He wanted *her* to be part of the win.

That took a moment to sink in. He cared about her. More than he should, obviously, given the way she'd bailed on him with no notice. But he could have sworn she was different from most of the people he saw socially.

She reminded him of Helena, solid, grounded, dependable.

He frowned. Abrienda definitely had a sense of duty and integrity. She'd have told him she was changing places with Teresa. If he hadn't been blind sided by her defection, he'd have picked up on the sense of wrongness about all of this.

"Oooo, you look upset," Teresa said, coming to stand beside him, resting a hand on his arm. "You're winning, so what's wrong?"

"Nothing."

But something was nagging at him. This morning's actions did not sound like the Abrienda he'd grown to know and care for.

"So tell me about this long jump. Do we fly all day?" she asked.

"We'll set down whenever we need fuel, then resume. We go as long as the propane lasts, or daylight ends, whichever comes first."

She glanced at the tanks.

"Did you bring lunch?" she asked.

"The ground crew has it."

"They will be there?"

He nodded. "Who do you think has the tanks to change out?"

The radio crackled.

"Boss, you have a problem," Manuel said.

Domingo picked up the mike.

"Go ahead."

He looked back at the other balloon. It followed faithfully, maybe five miles behind. A comfortable distance given the steady winds and lack of radical weather change.

"Philipe called. He said some woman called him saying she was part of our crew and abandoned in some small town and demanded he get her home."

"She should have thought of that before backing out of the race," Domingo said.

So she'd burned her bridges and hadn't thought about how she'd return home. Not his problem.

Yet he knew it was. He would never abandon anyone without a way for them to return home, especially Abrienda.

Especially Abrienda.

Domingo turned to look at Teresa. She wasn't the woman he wanted with him; Abrienda was. He'd known that earlier. Which was why it all felt wrong. He should have stormed up to her room and forced her to finish the race. He wanted her in on the victory.

"Actually she told him *you* had stranded her there and that she has no money."

Teresa was staring fixedly at the other balloon.

Suddenly everything became clear. He turned his head slowly and pierced her with a glare.

"What have you done?"

Chapter Twelve

Abrienda stood by the window in her room and waited. She'd done all she could. Henrico was checking on car services, air transportation from a private plane or bus transportation. She didn't care how she got there, she just wanted to go home.

Worst-case scenario, she'd stay in the hotel on Domingo's money until her brother returned home and could wire transfer her some money.

But she hoped Henrico would manage to find a way for her to get home before then. She didn't want Jose to worry if he arrived home before she did.

Her emotions went from anger to sadness at the way the race had ended for her. She'd known nothing lasting would come of the time spent with Domingo, but had hoped for a few more days. Even her fear of heights had diminished. With other things to think about, she could push that away and deal with soaring in the balloon.

For several wonderful days, she'd shared experiences with one of Barcelona's most eligible bachelors. Even dreamed that he'd fall for her. How absurd.

He was gorgeous; she was average. He was wealthy; she definitely was not. He liked dangerous sports; she liked sunning at the beach. He didn't want to marry; she wanted a marriage like her parents had. He didn't want children.

Abrienda thought about that. Eventually she'd like to have children. However, after the responsibility of raising her brother, she'd like a few years to enjoy being a couple, able to take trips on the spur of the moment, plan events with friends, without the worry of child care.

Not that Domingo had given so much as a hint that he'd ever see himself in that role. Unsurprising really, when his style was much more of the no-ties, no-commitments variety. Was Domingo even now kissing Teresa? Was one woman so interchangeable with another?

She frowned and turned away from the window and those depressing thoughts. He'd never promised her anything. He had no obligation to her, except to get her home.

And she'd make sure he never had a clue she'd fallen for him. Nor anyone else, either. It'd be her secret forever.

Pacing her room, the luxury was wasted on her. The best aspect was that it was large enough so she had more steps to make before turning to retrace them.

How dare he flit off without a word. Had he been afraid she'd refuse to let Teresa take her place? Maybe cause a scene?

She doubted it. Domingo didn't appear afraid of anything. And certainly not some heated words from a rival's irate PA.

Tears threatened. She shook her head. She was *not* going to cry over anyone or anything, especially Domingo Ortego. She'd done her best, even when she hadn't wanted to be there. So now she'd gotten her wish. She was going home.

Be careful what you wish for. The old phrase came to mind.

Snatching up her bag, she left the room. She'd wait in the lobby. She was tired of her own company, tired of her thoughts, tired of waiting. She'd at least see some activity in the lobby.

Stopping at the desk to let them know she wasn't in her room and would take calls here, she went to sit down. There were magazines on the tables. She leafed through a couple, but the photographs and articles didn't hold her interest.

What was taking Henrico so long? Granted this small town was off the beaten path, but surely it had interaction with the rest of Spain. How much longer?

It was almost noon when Henrico called back.

"I have hired a private car from San Sebastian. The driver will be there in the early afternoon. You'll be back home late tonight. The costs will be paid on our account. You get to deal with Vincente on this one."

"Thank you. Vincente got me into this, so he can settle the accounts with Ortego. I'll be back in the office tomorrow."

And give serious thought to changing jobs. She refused to be some pawn to be picked up and put down at the whim of hardheaded businessmen. For a moment she almost couldn't decide which one she was more angry with: Vincente or Domingo.

She left her bag with the bell captain and went to walk around the town and to get some lunch. It was early, but she didn't want to miss the car when it arrived. She'd given the doorman strict instructions about the car service. He was to make sure they waited for her if they came before she returned.

Since she hadn't eaten today, she ordered a large lunch at

a sidewalk café and enjoyed the sunshine and the quiet little town. Then she walked back to the hotel.

To her surprise she saw the chase team truck parked in front. She quickened her pace. Maybe they'd come back for her. Maybe she could still be part of the team and in on the finish. Maybe she'd misconstrued everything.

Abrienda stopped dead upon entering the lobby. Domingo paced the area in front of the desk.

"Domingo?" she exclaimed. "What on earth are you doing here?"

He turned and crossed the lobby, taking her in his arms and hugging her tightly.

"You should be in the balloon. Did something happen?" she asked, muffled against his chest.

He put her at arm's length and looked at her.

"Did you think I had deliberately left you behind?" he asked.

She blinked. That wasn't an answer to her question.

"Well, here I am and everyone else is gone. What was I to think?"

"That I would never do such a thing."

This was wrong. He should be miles away, airborne, outdistancing her boss. What was he doing back here at the hotel?

"Why aren't you in the air?" she repeated.

"I was, until I found out Teresa had pulled that stunt. She told me when she came down to join the crew early this morning that you had convinced her to take your place. That you hated being in the balloon. It made sense. You've made no secret of the fact you don't like heights."

She drew herself up.

"I would have told you myself if I weren't going today."

"Yeah, I got that about an hour ago. I wasn't thinking straight. I was so mad you had backed out and sent Teresa in as a substitute."

"I did *not,*" she said, outraged.

"I know that now. And I'd have known it early this morning if I had been thinking sensibly. But I wasn't, only reacting."

"I don't understand. Dom, where is the balloon?"

"In a field somewhere about an hour from here."

He waved one hand.

"What are you *doing*? Vincente will get ahead. You have to get back."

"He can win the damn race. It's you I'm worried about."

"Me?"

Abrienda didn't know what to do, how to react. Her heart was pounding so hard she couldn't even think.

"I'd never leave you stranded, Abrienda. Didn't I say I'd get you home safely?"

"Yes, but I thought that meant you wouldn't let me fall out of the balloon."

He brushed her hair from the side of her face.

"I meant I'd take you home. You could have trusted me."

His touch felt heavenly. She tried to figure out what was going on.

"And how would that have changed anything? I slept through until the sun woke me. You were gone. When I didn't come down to the lobby, why didn't you come get me? You had no qualms about doing that in Barcelona."

"I regret not coming to your room and demanding you get up and go with us. It was my first instinct and I should have followed through on it. But I didn't learn until a short time ago that Teresa had called down to cancel your wake-up call. You were still planning to go with me, weren't you? It wasn't your idea to send Teresa in your place."

"I would never have done such a thing," she reiterated, hope finally blossoming. He hadn't abandoned her, at least not deliberately.

"It seemed logical, I mean Teresa's taking your place. No more fear during the day. No more camping out or dealing with a storm. You'd return to your home and not care a bit about the outcome of the stupid race." He frowned. "Anyway, it all made sense at 5:00 a.m."

"It *is* a stupid race. And you're going to lose it if you don't get going," she urged.

"Not going to happen until we get this cleared up. You are more important than a hundred races. In fact, I think you are the most important thing I have in my life right now."

She blinked. "What do you mean?"

She licked suddenly dry lips.

"I mean you're more important than besting Alvarez. More important than finishing the race. I've fallen for you, Abrienda. You're unlike any woman I know, in a very special way. Only, I didn't realize it until Teresa tried to explain why she'd pulled that stunt. All I could think of was you here alone. And that you might think I left you. It doesn't take much to imagine what you must have been feeling. While I know you are capable, I feel responsible for you and I probably always will. I would never do anything to deliberately hurt you."

His hands cupped her face. The lobby faded. Abrienda focused on the dark eyes that gazed so warmly down into hers.

"You hardly know me," she whispered. "I'm no one's responsibility."

"What I do know I love. And I hope the rest will follow as the years unfold. We've been together more in the last few days than many people are before they get engaged. I want that for us. I never thought I'd ask, but I want you to marry me, Abrienda Delmarico. Show me a family like I've never known. Take me into yours. I want to know Jose. To be included in family events. Learn what we can explore together, build a life that will give us all the happy memories we can ever want. As I drove like a madman to get back here before you could leave, I realized the crushing disappointment I felt this morning was because I thought you didn't want to be with me. But I remembered every moment we've been together on the drive back, and I'm hoping I saw signs that might mean you care for me as well."

"I'm not sophisticated or cosmopolitan," she protested, even though she wanted to bite her tongue.

He knew that. If he was still asking her to marry him, she should ignore all the reasons why not and accept. Was there anything she wanted more?

"No, but I think you're perfect the way you are. You're honest, passionate regarding things you care about and have a strong sense of duty. I'm fascinated by the way your mind works, by the ideas you come up with. By how your eyes sparkle and your entire face seems to shine when you smile. I love you, Abrienda. I didn't know the balloon trip would ever end up this way. Every spin of the tires had me remembering every second of our time together. The special bond that grew almost without my knowing it. Only when I thought you'd left did I realize how important it was for you to stay. Say you'll share your life with me for the next fifty or sixty years—or longer."

"I don't know, Domingo."

"We can have as long an engagement as you want. Let you get to know me. Let me get to know you even more. But consider the time we've spent together. More than most couples who date a few hours one or two nights a week. I've seen how you handle adversity. How you're brave when needed. I know you stand up for your rights. I don't think Vincente will ever be quite the same again."

She laughed as the delight filled her heart. Dare she believe he meant it? Her heart swelled with love. "You do me great honor, Domingo Ortego. I would love to be your wife. I love you. I—"

Her words were lost as his mouth covered hers when he pulled her into his embrace. The thrill of his kiss was only increased by the knowledge that she would have kisses like this for the rest of her life. Abrienda felt as if she were soaring.

Epilogue

Domingo escorted Abrienda to their table. He introduced her to the other members of the Barcelona Business Alliance seated at the table and met their guests in exchange.

Seated, she smiled at him. He had known she would look beautiful in burgundy. The dress fit her trim figure perfectly, the long lines making her seem taller and even more slender. Her dark hair was done in some elaborate upswept design. One he would delight in taking down later when he escorted her home.

She leaned forward. "Nervous?" she asked.

"Not a bit. Should I be?"

She wrinkled her nose at him.

"I did as you asked and didn't say a word to Vincente. He's planning to gloat, you know. I still think we could have had a shot at the distance. He couldn't have been that far ahead if we'd dashed back to the balloon."

"Relax. The others had a great time taking rides and there will be more opportunities to challenge your boss."

"Soon-to-be-former boss. Honestly, if I have another day like today, I'd likely deck him."

He laughed and Abrienda smiled, happy every time she heard his deep laughter.

The last two weeks had flown by. Jose had been over the top when he learned of his sister's engagement, corralling Domingo every time he came to the apartment to question him on everything from lighter-than-air travel, to scuba diving, to mountain climbing. She was almost afraid her studious brother might take a different turn in college.

They had dinner together almost every evening at their flat. Dom became engulfed in their lives and seemed to enjoy every minute.

Abrienda loved the few evenings he insisted on taking her out. But unlike the past, Domingo kept their dating secret. There were no reporters with snippets in the newspaper, no photographs splashed across the society pages.

They talked about everything under the sun, and she fell more and more in love.

Last weekend he'd taken her and Jose out on his sailboat. Heavenly. She definitely preferred sailing on the sea than in the air.

Her only regret was he'd lost the race. Sure there'd be other times, but she knew how much Domingo had wanted to beat Vincente. She wanted him to have everything he wanted. It seemed fair, he'd given her everything with his love.

After the sumptuous dinner, the president of the alliance rose to address those present. The speaker gave his speech. Applause was polite. Then the president introduced Vincente.

Domingo was sitting casually in his chair, watching with amused eyes. Abrienda was nervous as she waited for her boss to begin his bragging winner's speech. She wished he'd get it over with. She wanted to jump up and defend Dom, to explain they'd been leading but he'd stopped for something he considered even more important.

Vincente rambled on for several minutes, ending with the announcement that he'd won and Domingo Ortego owed him fifty thousand Euros.

Heads turned, smiled appeared. Domingo stood and reached for Abrienda.

"Come with me," he said.

The move surprised her and obviously Vincente. She hoped she didn't look as dumbfounded as she felt.

They climbed the few steps to the platform and walked to the center where the podium and microphone were.

Vincente smiled at Domingo, gloating every moment.

Domingo walked up to him and offered his hand.

"Congratulations, Vincente, your balloon went the farthest."

While not speaking into the mike, his voice carried.

Vincente faltered a moment and then nodded and shook his hand. He glanced at Abrienda, puzzled.

Domingo took out a check from his pocket, looked at it and then turned to the audience.

"As Vincente explained, we had a bet. He went the distance and I have a check for fifty thousand Euros to give to him."

He handed Vincente the check. The audience applauded. Vincente beamed with satisfaction. He loved to be the center of attention.

Domingo pulled Abrienda up beside him and turned back to the mike.

"But Vincente didn't win as much as I did. I found the love of my life on that balloon race and I'm delighted to share with each of you tonight that Abrienda Delmarico has promised to marry me. She thought the bet a stupid action between two wealthy men. There were many better uses for fifty thousand Euros, she said. I promised her I would turn over the winnings to her favorite charity if we won. Since I feel I won the biggest prize of all, I have a check for fifty thousand Euros made payable to The Sisters of Charity's Children's Home."

He pulled out the check and handed it to her.

"In honor of her parents, who are unable to see the happiness their daughter has brought me because of their untimely deaths nine years ago. I thank them in absentia for giving me Abrienda."

Abrienda took the check, her eyes swimming with tears.

"It's I who have won," she whispered as happiness bubbled over. She so loved this man.

The applause was heartfelt. But when Domingo took her into his arms to kiss her, the Barcelona Business Alliance went wild with a standing ovation. The first in the history of the organization.

Domingo hugged her close, saying over the sound of the crowd, for her alone, "We know the truth—Vincente loses. We win."

Did you enjoy this story?
If so, you may enjoy the next book in
Viva Espana series, **Alicante Moonlight.**

www.ingramcontent.com/pod-product-compliance
Lightning Source LLC
Chambersburg PA
CBHW051648260626
47170CB00004B/1388

* 9 7 8 1 9 6 0 7 9 5 4 4 1 *